The Disappearance of Cyrum T. Washington

By

Michael ("Mick") J. Zimmerle

Copyright @ 2002 by Michael J. Zimmerle

Published by Trade Name: Baby Boomer Mysteries

ISBN 0-9703943-2-2

Purpose of books:

To spur the interest of children to read, and to teach valuable lessons using subtle themes and adult role models.

Titles of the books in Baby Boomer Mysteries:

The Church Tower Mystery
Theme: The inner person is important. Outside appearances can be deceptive.

The Mystery of the Gold Double Eagle
Theme: Forgiveness is essential for children and adults alike.

The Disappearance of Cyrum T. Washington
Theme: Hope

The Mystery of the Lost Masterpiece (Coming next)
Theme: Restoration/Wholeness

To my wife for keeping me encouraged and excited about writing.

Thanks to Carolyn Yankel for her editing expertise.

Thanks to Maida Chaney for her editing and evaluation.

Thanks to the Dayton Montgomery County Public Library for the use of the photo's of the library and canal boat in Chapter 4.

Thanks to Nick Beigel for the photos of his store and information on diamonds.

Thanks to Joseph Masterson for the photos of his market.

To order more books browse our Web address;

WWW.BABYBOOMERMYSTERIES.COM

E-Mail: Info@babyboomermysteries.com

Note to the reader:

This story is fictional.
The city of Dayton, Ohio is used as a backdrop to the mystery, to give the story realism.

Facts that are true:
Tuskegee Airmen were black pilots in World War II trained in Alabama at Tuskegee Institute and Tuskegee Army Air Field.

Paul Laurence Dunbar is a black poet from Dayton.

Woodland Cemetery has famous people buried on the premises: the Wright Brothers, Paul Laurence Dunbar, and a host of others.

The photo of the bell tower in Chapter 9 is the Carillon Bell Tower in Dayton, Ohio. The park restores historical buildings, such as Newcom Tavern, that dates back to 1796. The Wright Flyer III airplane is there, donated by Orville Wright.

Hans von Ohain did live in Dayton Ohio in 1957. He was the German physicist who invented the first turbojet engine that flew in 1939.

Oscar Beigel's Jewelers is still in business today.

The Midnight Market is on 3rd street and Linden Avenue and is still doing business.

Contents

Chapter   Page

1.   Tin CanMan 6
2.   Strangers Only Once 18
3.   The Field Trip 31
4.   Library Clues 47
5.   Street People Talk 62
6.   The Bridge 81
7.   The Pump Station 95
8.   The Jeweler 104
9.   Carillon Bells 115
10.   Duck Lady 132
11.   Wympee's Restaurant 141
12.   Cemetery 156
13.   The Exchange 171
14.   The Reunion 188

Photographs by the author

Chapter 1

Tin Can Man

Squeek! Squeek, squeek! The unusual sound was coming from the alley behind the garage.

"What is that noise?" Tait thought to himself as the rythmic squeek continued nagging him to investigate. He ran full speed between the garage and the aluminum wire fence toward the alley and out the gate when he rammed his head into the side of a man and got smashed to the asphalt. The collision took away Tait's breath.

The black man looming over him made Tait feel like a small bug rolling around on the ground. The dark tattered suit with patches of tin can labels sewn into the fabric made the man appear alien. The Campbell's Soup and baked bean labels were weird yet curiously fascinating. A fisherman's hat, with lures attached, covered the man's head. A large burlap sack slung over his shoulder bulged with pop bottles.

Tait lifted his back off the ground, belly up, and moved awkwardly backwards. Panicky, his eyes never left the strange sight. He righted himself and bolted through the gate. Resisting a glance back he focused on speed as he heard a deep laugh behind him. Halfway to the house, Tait regained his composure.

"Be tough," he thought to himself. "Your brother Joe wouldn't run." Tait got a determined look on his face and turned around. He stepped up onto the window sill of the garage and up the spouting to the roof. He crawled on his belly along the peak of the roof toward the alley. Perched at the edge he lifted his head and there below was the trashpicker examining a wood rocking chair, broken where the curved piece meets the leg.

Suddenly, the black man turned around and looked up straight at Tait. Preparing to escape, Tait's muscles stiffened, but he didn't move.

"There's no need to be afraid. I'm just looking for things I can fix like this chair here," he said softly, re-examining the break in the wood. "What do you think? Do you think I can fix it?"

Tait, caught off guard by the question, thought for a moment. "My dad could fix it," he said convincingly.

"Well then, I'll give it a try." The man placed the rocker into his cart and pushed the cart forward a little. Squeek, squeek went the left front wheel.

The cart was a large, wooden, handmade buggy. The sides were painted white. A long horizontal, bright red, bar was used to maneuver the buggy. The words "By Request" were painted diagonally along the sides in black letters. In front, the cart had small wagon wheels, while its back wheels were large bicycle tires. The black man would lean on the push-bar handle to raise the front of the cart to go up curbs and maneuver the cart right or left. The cart was filled with interesting things. A tricycle with one wheel missing, a small wagon, a broken radio, an old table lamp with a busted shade, plastic folding chairs and a small table, and a toilet tank, all piled high but methodically placed, in that self-styled shopping cart.

"What do you do with all that junk?" Tait asked.

Embarrased the man smiled and chuckled to himself, "Acutally I'm doing this on a bet. I'm taking the place of a poor man named Dennis Tucker, a local handyman. I dressed up his cart a little and I'm sort of doing some shopping for him."

"Does he dress like you?" Tait asked amazed.

The black man replied humorously, " Yes, strangely enough, the man wears this costume. I barrowed it. The neighbors call him Tin Can Man. Halloween is tonight and this getup kinda fits the occasion don't you think?"

"Yeah! It's scary," Tait admitted. "What does Dennis Tucker do with all the junk?"

"He sells the scrap iron and copper. He fixes toys, furniture and other things to sell. Well most of it. Some of it he give away to poor folks."

"Poorer than him?" Tait ask in disbelief.

"Yep! Like this tricycle," he said lifting it out of the cart. "He will fix it up and give it to a youngster. In fact, I think I got something in here for you."

Tait was puzzled. "What could he have in the pile of junk for me?" he thought.

The man dug around and pulled out a sling shot. It was hand carved from a fork of a tree branch. A super large rubber band with a leather strap in the middle made it the best sling shot Tait had ever seen. The man stooped over and picked up a piece of gravel from the alley and placed it into the leather strap of the sling. He aimed and hit a trash can thirty yards away. The ding sound of the rock against the can proved the value of the weapon.

"Do you want it?" he asked raising it above his head in Tait's direction.

"Sure," Tait replied and reached down from the peak of the roof and snatched it from the man's hand.

"Enjoy it," the black man said and continued down the alley stopping occasionally to sift out things to keep from unwanted trash. Tait listened to the fading squeek, squeek of the trashpicker's cart and took in the sounds of the fall season.

A whirlwind of leaves funneled upward and settled into a corner by a shed. The damp cold of autumn seemed to accompany Halloween every year and it again reminded Tait that today at dusk was "beggers night". The alley seemed empty now that the stranger was gone. Tait's mother called him back into the house. He had missed a customer and had to deliver the newspaper immediately.

Tait, not wanting to be late for trick-or-treat hurried along crunching his bicycle through crimson leaves piled high along the curbs and delivered the paper. Tait noticed the scary faces of Jack-0-lanterns glowing on porches and the smell of wood burning in usually unlit fire places. People were busy making preperations for the young candy shoppers to come later that night. The chill air brought hot apple cider to mind and he knew his mother would have some waiting when he got home.

"Halloween is going to be fun," he thought and couldn't wait to tell his best friend Marcus about his encounter with a man dressed in tin can labels.

Marcus insisted on scouting out the alleys before

dressing in their costumes so he could get a look. Darkness set in and they failed to spot the strange garbage picker despite rumors that he was sighted just a few blocks away.

The people were generous. Most houses along Tait's street had their front porch lights on, which signaled they were giving out candy. Every year some kid would excitedly report that Oscar Beigel, the jeweler on Xenia Avenue, was passing out dimes to the "Trick or Treaters", but you had to get there early. And every year Tait was disappointed when he only got a Clark bar.

Tait used a large brown "A&P" grocery bag to collect his candy. The bag gradually grew heavy with Hershey chocolate bars, Tootsie Rolls, Cracker Jacks and an occasional apple that Tait liked least of all. Tait always got an eerie feeling looking through the holes of his mask. It distorted his view of things. The moonlight and the cool autumn breeze made things look and feel ghostly. Tait's hearing seemed more alert to the noises of the night.

Don Dorfer, a high school kid, swore he saw Tin Can Man roaming in alleys nearby. The darkness and its noises, and now the sighting of the unusual garbage picker in the neighborhood, made this Halloween particularly panicky. Most kids stayed close to their friends for protection.

The next day, after tossing a baseball for awhile on the playground, Tait and Marcus walked home contented, eating chocolate bars. Tait and Marcus noticed a man walk up to Tait's house and knock on the door. The man had not shaved in weeks, displaying a wild unkept beard, a scraggly mustache and oily hair too messy to go unnoticed. The pants he wore were wrinkled as if he had slept in them. His gray winter coat was dirty, with dried mud on the back.

"Hey Marcus," Tait commented. "What do you think that bum wants?"

"Candy," Marcus quipped. "He still thinks it's Halloween." Both boys laughed.

Tait's mom appeared at the door. Tait could see her point to the porch step. The man sat down and waited. He calmly pulled out a cigarette and smoked, acting as if he lived there. A short time later, Tait's mom reappeared with a lunch bag. The man thanked her and left. The man passed Tait and Marcus on the sidewalk, giving them no notice.

"Pew," cried Marcus holding his nose. "The man smells

like a bottle of booze."

"Let's track him," Tait suggested.

"Okay," agreed Marcus, and they casually tossed a baseball between them as they strolled down the sidewalk, far behind the man. Marcus ran out into the middle of the street and yelled for a long throw from Tait to disguise the fact that they were actually following the man.

After several blocks, the man stepped into the street and threw the lunch bag down the storm sewer at its opening along the curb.

"Hey, did you see that Marcus?" curiously whispered Tait. "He just threw away my mom's sandwiches. Why would he do that?"

"He did it because he is a drunk. I bet he asked your mom for some money saying he was hungry. He really wanted to buy whiskey."

"Now I know why Mom never gives money," Tait said, understanding his mother's wisdom.

The boys followed the man to the railroad tracks along Fifth Street where he reclined on the grassy knoll along the tracks.

"He's a train hopper!" Marcus smirked. "Do you think he is a fugitive running from the law?"

"He's a bum is all I know," Tait replied. "Do you know that nuclear shipments are on some of these trains?"

"Really!"

"Really, that's why the railroad police guard the tracks," Tait informed Marcus.

"I didn't know there were railroad police."

"My dad says it's illegal and incredibly dangerous to walk the tracks," reported Tait. "Rail cops used to be famous in the 1930s. A lot of the tramps were outlaws. In those days, the cops and the rail-riding hoboes had gun battles. Cops would shoot hoboes from moving trains."

"Hey, that bum is getting up. Let's investigate," Marcus whispered, while squatting down below the hill.

The train hopper disappeared around the corner of a warehouse next to the tracks. Tait and Marcus ran to get closer, and then turned the corner of the warehouse.

"Got you!" clucked the man in a loud, victorious voice as he tugged on Tait's jacket lifting him up onto his toes. "So you two kids are following me. Why?"

Tait tried to break loose but failed. Marcus yelled out, "Let him go, you big jerk!"

"I'll let you go," he said, throwing Tait to the ground. "Next time I'll cut your throat if I see you following me. Get the message kid?" he growled angrily.

"I get the message. We're out of here," Tait announced. "Come on, Marcus."

The boys returned home and told Tait's mom the whole story.

Sunday morning came, and that meant getting up early to deliver newspapers in the dark of the night. As usual, Tait rode his bike a mile down the alleyways to the branch garage where the paper truck dropped off the bundles of the Dayton Daily News. Sunday papers were big. Tait's bike had back saddlebags as well as a front bag on the handlebars. All the bags were stuffed full. After papers were delivered, he liked to meet his friends at the diner by the railroad tracks on Fifth Street. It was an odd shaped building with one wall following the tracks. It looked like half of a building turned sideways. When a train went by, the whole building shook with each passing car. Tait sat on a counter stool and drank chocolate milk until Marcus arrived. Afterwards, he played pinball with his friends for a nickel a game.

Shortly after dawn, Tait left to return home. The sun was still rising, the morning doves sat on the high power lines and cooed. Cupping his hands together with his thumbs to form a whistle hole, Tait blew sounds like that of a pop bottle whistle. Tait could imitate the morning dove's call. He always chuckled when a dove cooed back.

Riding his bike with no hands while cooing to the doves, Tait heard a man yell out asking to buy a paper. Tait slowed down to reach into his bag. A shock wave went through Tait's head from a hard blow, the man flattening him to the pavement. With his knee in Tait's back, the attacker picked Tait's wallet from his back pocket. He pushed Tait's head to the ground. Tait squirmed enough to get a look and recognized the derelict as the one his mom had given food. The man's face revealed that he, too, recognized Tait. From inside his overcoat, the man pulled out a knife.

Chapter 2

Strangers only once

Suddenly a tall black figure stood over both of them. The bum looked up just in time to see the fist coming. Tait heard the thud of the collision of knuckles against the jaw bone of the derelict. The bum fell sideways off Tait and rolled over in pain hiding the knife with his body.

"Don't ever touch this boy again," rang loud in the still of the morning. "Get out of here!" boomed the words in a slow deliberate voice.

"I hear you," said the bum, getting up slowly while

wiping his bloody mustache and mouth with his left shirtsleeve. With his face down he fingered the knife for a moment and then cautiously backed away. With a sudden jerk he darted away, crossed the tracks and disappeared down the incline on the other side.

Tait was on one elbow looking up at the black man he met in the alley a few days before. A brown suit, white shirt and bright red pastel tie replaced the tattered suit with the tin can labels.

"Are you alright?" the black man asked as he helped Tait to his feet.

"Yeah, thanks."

"That derelict may follow you. Keep a watch out."

"What about you?" asked Tait. "He may try and kill you."

"I'm sure he would if he had the chance. I'm used to it. I always have to be careful in a white neighborhood You are not used to being hunted. I'll have to give you some tips on how to stay alive."

Tait thought about that for a moment. This was serious. The derelict could pop out of nowhere any time and get him.

"This man is dangerous," emphasized the black man. "I know. I could feel his hate when he looked at me."

Tait tried to pick up his bike but it was awkward and unmanageable.

"Looks like the fork is bent and the handlebars are out of position. The man put the front wheel between his legs and groaned while he muscled the handlebars back into their proper place. "There," he said, as he pushed the bike into Tait's hands. "That's good enough for you to ride until you get the fork replaced."

"Thanks," said Tait as he straddled the seat and wiggled the handlebars, testing the movement of the front wheel. Gazing at the man he asked. "What's your name?"

"Cyrum," the black man replied. "What's yours?"

"Tait," he answered. "Tait Bolinger."

"Come on, I'll drive you home. The bum might want revenge and follow you."

Tait rode slow and wobbly as Cyrum walked alongside to his automobile. Cyrum opened the trunk and placed the bike inside and tied the trunk lid down with twine.

"Next time, leave a little room to escape until you know a stranger's intentions," Cyrum instructed. "Go ahead and get in the back."

"He was on me before I knew what happened."

"Yeah, you were pretty well had."

Another man who was in the front seat of the car on the passengers side got out and let Tait get in the rear seat.

"This is my brother Jim," Cyrum explained. We are on our way to chapel on the Air Force Base. I'm speaking today," Cyrum explained.

"Hi," Tait said.

"Lucky for you my brother came along. Looked like you were about to be done in," Jim said.

"That's not luck," Cyrum interrupted. "God protects his people. This is what I'm speaking on today. I'm going to talk about trusting the Lord and the importance of hope."

"Are you a preacher?" Tait asked intrigued.

"No, I'm a retired Tuskegee Airman," said Cyrum proudly. "The Lord has helped me through many a trial.

"What's a Tuskegee?"

"Tuskegee is a school in Alabama. Hundreds of black

aviators were trained to fly during World War II at that Institute and the nearby Army Air Field. Those were hard days. Those days made men out of boys. My closest friend Dan Thomas was killed in an air battle."

"Wow! I had no idea you were a pilot. Why don't you fly planes?"

"I do fly planes. I just retired from the Air Force. I'm seeking a commercial air lines job now. I've been fishing and enjoying life at the moment and trying to convince my brother to attend church and accept the Lord."

"Looks like Jim is going to church today. He is in the car," Tait said wrinkling up his forehead like it was a foregone conculsion..

"Jim's in the car because he lost the bet," Cyrum said as he looked over at his brother.

"What bet?" Tait asked.

"I told you when I met you in the alley that I was pushing Dennis Tucker's cart. I walked in his shoes so to speak."

"Oh yeah!," Tait said nodding his head.

"Cyrum talks about his war years all the time," Jim

said to further explain the bet. "I said Dennis Tucker had more courage than Cyrum. Dennis Tucker pushes his cart through the white neighborhoods. Now that takes guts for a black man. I bet Cyrum he didn't have the courage to do it."

"I agreed to do it on one condition. Jim would have to go to church with me on Sunday."

"To make things a little tougher, I made Cyrum wear the tin can suit being it was Halloween," Jim said laughing. "I couldn't believe he did it. The man's got my respect."

"I flew over a hundred combat missions and it takes a stunt like this to get my brothers respect. What do you think about that, Tait?"

"I think Jim's jealous and just tried to get your dander up," Tait replied. Jim turned around and stared at Tait but didn't say anything. He knew it was true.

"Well, it cost him. Now he has to go to church after having sworn he would never go," Cyrum said with a smile. "People wear masks of smiles and tears to hide their inner thoughts. Did you know that, Tait?"

"Yeah. Is that what Jim did?"

"Heck no. Cyrum brags all the time that's all," Jim said.

"Dayton has a poet who wrote about wearing masks. Do you want to hear it?"

"Sure," Tait said interested.

"'We Wear the Mask,' by Paul Laurence Dunbar," proclaimed Cyrum, raising his voice high into the air.

"We wear the mask that grins and lies,

It hides our cheeks and shades our eyes,

This debt we pay to human guile;

With torn and bleeding hearts we smile,

And mouth with myriad subtleties.

Why should the world be overwise,

In counting all our tears and sighs?

Nay, let them see only us, while

We wear the mask.

We smile, but, O great Christ, our cries

To thee from tortured souls arise.

We sing, but oh the clay is vile

Beneath our feet, and long the mile:
But let the world dream otherwise,
We wear the mask!"

Tait gave directions to his house as Cyrum turned the corners without stopping his recital. When it was over Tait clapped. That's really good," Tait said.

Stopping in front of the house Cyrum got out and retrieved Tait's bike and said, "Every man must go through the fire of life, the fire that makes a man a man. It is the inner man that counts. Remember that."

"Is that what the war taught you," Tait asked.

"Oh yes!" Cyrum said clearly and definitively as they stood by the side of the car. "Being a pilot makes a man out of you."

"Here we go again," his brother said out the window. "Another war story."

Why, I remember Dan and I escorting a formation of B-24s. We were flying P-51s, fighter aircraft. We always stayed close off their wings about a hundred yards."

Tait listened, enchanted at the excitement in Cyrum's

voice over recalling his war days.

"Why did you have to escort them?" inquired Tait. "They had machine guns on their planes too, didn't they?"

"Yes, bombers had machine guns. The bombers were slow. They bombed German factories, railroad yards, oil refineries and so they were targets for the German guns and fighter planes. It was our job to protect them so that they could complete their mission."

"Your plane was a lot faster, right?"

"Right. Our fighters were faster and more maneuverable. The pilots in the bombers loved to see us off their wings. It gave them a sense of security. They would often look out their windows and give us a thumbs up."

"I wish I could be a fighter pilot."

"You can if you work hard."

"What happened to the German fighters that were coming after you?"

"Actually there were no German fighters on that mission. An alien aircraft joined the bomber squadron.

"What do you mean by an alien aircraft?"

"The Germans were clever. They would rebuild American aircraft that crash landed in their territory. They would join up with American bomber formations.

"Pretty tricky."

"I gave him some bursts from my canons, and warned him to turn back and that I would escort him. I didn't want him using his guns on our bombers."

"Then what happened?"

"I flew so close the pilot could see my eyes. I scared him with my grin."

"Did you kill him?"

"No. Dan and I escorted him back to the airfield where he was arrested and made a prisoner of war."

"Wow, did you get a medal for that?"

"No. Not that time, but I do have medals. Maybe some day I'll show you. It's time I let you go."

A car passed with the window down and Tait heard taunts, loud and clear. Cyrum gave it little notice. He had heard them thousands of times before.

"I'm going on a field trip tomorrow," said Tait.

"You are? Where?"

"To the Dayton Art Institute. The Hope Diamond is on display. It's worth a lot of money."

"Yes, diamonds usually are."

"My teacher preached half the day on Friday about rules and regulations."

"Like what?"

"About getting on and off the bus orderly, and staying in line, and no talking in the museum except to ask questions."

"That makes sense."

"The principal came into our classroom with her usual bad temper. 'I just came to remind all of you that you will be representing the school'," Tait said imitating the principal's mannerisms and stern voice. " 'So be on your best behavior if you want to see the Hope Diamond'."

Cyrum laughed at Tait's impersonation of the principal.

"Did you know the Hope Diamond was found in India?" Tait asked, like a kid trying to get one up on an adult.

"No, I didn't".

"King Louis XIV of France bought the diamond. It is intense blue," Tait pointed out. "It was stolen once. It was found in London years later."

"Maybe I should go see this Hope Diamond."

"Yeah, why don't you?"

"How did it get to be called the Hope Diamond?" Cyrum inquired.

"A guy bought it named Hope, like Bob Hope, except his name was Henry, I think. Some guy in the U.S. owns the diamond now, and is showing it at exhibits all over the world?"

"So it's being shown at the Dayton Art Institute?" Cyrum questioned, interested.

"That's right and I'm going tomorrow to see it."

They both saw it. A face peering around the corner of the school building across the street.

"I think I see the train hopping bum. He followed us," Tait informed Cyrum.

Cyrum stared but admitted he couldn't tell for sure if it was the bum. "I think I'll go tomorrow to the museum. I could use a little culture. See ya later," Cyrum said and got in his car.

Tait watched the car fade away in the distance until out of sight. Tait wondered if Cyrum really would be at the museum tomorrow. He gazed over one more time where he had seen the transient whiskey-drinking bum and then went into the house.

Chapter 3

The Field Trip

A breeze of cold November air hit Tait in the face as he got off the bus in front of the Dayton Art Institute. Marcus started toward the big glass doors only to have Mrs. Norton call him back in line.

"No talking, just get in line," the teacher ordered. Another bus pulled up and parked. Tait saw his younger sister Katie get off. That class formed a line parallel to Tait's. They went into the museum as more buses pulled up.

"This may be the first and last time you children will ever see a large diamond like this. Diamonds this size are rarely seen except by kings and the very rich," the tour guide explained as the children formed a circle around the famous blue diamond on display.

Katie waved to Tait when she saw him. His class was up close to the display table. A glass covering locked to the table shielded the diamond from its spectators. A rope circled the display table creating a safe barrier from the crowd. Tait leaned against the rope to take a good look.

"Now everyone will get their chance to get a close look at the Hope Diamond. Just be patient. Don't push. Everyone must move slowly and keep the line moving. Circle the display table once and then proceed to another area of the museum to see the other exhibits," explained the tour guide. "A large blue Indian diamond, was taken to France in the 17th century. Years later it was stolen. King George IV of England died and the stone was found in his collection. Later the diamond was found in the gem collection of Henry Philip Hope. The stone has been called the Hope Diamond ever since.

Some boy was waving his arm to get the tour guide's attention and hit a girl in the head with his elbow. He shouted out the question. "How large was the biggest diamond ever found?'

"The biggest diamond ever found weighed over a pound. It was found in 1905 in South Africa. It was cut into nine large stones called the Stars of Africa."

"We heard all this already at school," Marcus said bored. He leaned against the rope and gazed at the diamond.

"It is pretty big," Tait said, "Isn't it.

"So who cares. I don't want to wear it. I'd rather have a baseball autographed by Yogi Berra."

Free to explore the rest of the museum, Katie joined Tait and Marcus, "How did you guys like it?" Katie asked.

"It's nice," said Tait "but not very useful."

"It's not a tool. It's a thing of beauty. I like it," Katie claimed.

"Let's run through the museum to see what we can find," Tait suggested.

Off they went, only to be told to slow down as they walked by one of the teachers. They entered a room full of huge oil paintings. One painting took up most of the wall, reaching ten feet high.

"Wow, these pictures are big," Marcus remarked.

"These are not pictures. Photos are pictures. These are oil paintings. These are old and cost a lot of money," Katie corrected. "These are from the age of realism. They look like they could be a photograph. Of course, photography wasn't invented until the nineteenth century."

"Oh brother! You're really getting into this museum stuff. Please don't bore me," Marcus said disgustedly. "Are there any mummies here?"

Tait stood for a moment gazing at details of a large oil painting and then announced, "I have to go to the restroom. Let's look for one."

They found a door in a cove that looked like part of a church. A stained glass window lit up the small area and the pillared entrance was shaped like a church doorway curved and pointed at the top. On the door was the word "Restroom" in black letters. They decided to enter.

To their surprise, a long poorly lighted hallway had two doors on the right side wall, one for men and one for women.   The old marble sinks and huge mirrors with fancy frames interested the boys as much as the blue diamond. The toilets flushed hard and loud, splashing water over the top of the rim.

"Oh shoot," cried Tait, "Now it looks like I wet my pants."

Marcus laughed hard when he saw the wet spot on Tait's pants.

They met Katie back at the cove below the stained glass window.

"Hey there, Tait. You learning anything?"

There stood proud and erect a good looking black man in a crisp white shirt and pressed tan pants.

"Cyrum! You came to the museum!" cried Tait.

"Marcus, this is Cyrum," introduced Tait.

"You got to be kidding. You're Tin Can Man?" Marcus repeated in disbelief.

"Just for a day," Tait corrected."Cyrum is a pilot."

"Cyrum T. Washington is the name," he said holding out his hand to Marcus.

Marcus shook Cyrum's hand, responding with, "I'm

Marcus Kenecki."

"Glad to meet you.

"I'm Katie Bolinger, Tait's sister," she said.

"Are you liking the art?" Cyrum asked.

"I like it," Katie answered enthusiastically. "The Hope Diamond is beautiful."

"Yeah, the diamond is something special."

"I like baseball better," Marcus retorted.

"Nothing wrong with baseball," agreed Cyrum.

"Tait told me you were a fighter pilot in World War II. Is that true?" asked Katie.

"Oh yes, it's true. Flew in Korea also."

"Do you have any medals?"

"Yes. I do. I have a medal for shooting down a jet."

"Wow, that must have been dangerous," she replied.

"Very dangerous. Many of my friends died in combat."

"Did you get hurt?" asked Katie.

"Only on the inside."

"What is war like?" Tait asked.

"Terrifying! Don't let anybody tell you different," he said sternly.

"How did you shoot down that jet?" Tait asked.

"The jet aircraft had just been developed by the Germans. In fact the turbojet engine was invented in 1939 by Hans von Ohain, a German physicist who lives in Dayton Ohio now."

"You've got to be kidding!" Marcus said unbelieving.

"No, I'm not kidding. He was not a Nazi. He is a very nice man. I met him. He works at Wright-Patterson Air Force Base."

"Wow! The Wright Brothers are from Dayton and Hans von Ohain lives in Dayton," Marcus said astounded.

"Marcus quit interrupting and let him finish the story," Tait said anxiously wanting to hear the rest.

"Jets could fly straight up and that's how I spotted the plane. I was flying escort for a group of bombers headed for Berlin when a formation of German planes were flying under our group."

"So you were in a dog fight?" Marcus interrupted.

"You bet ya. My plane was flying like this." Cyrum used his hands to illustrate. "The enemy was coming straight up after me, trying to get above me. He got behind me instead.

I spun out to the left, went down a bit, and then quickly up again and circled above him. He lost sight of me. He must of thought I went down. Looking for me, he came straight up again. We ended up flying straight at each other, nose to nose, about the distance of five or six football fields apart. Before he realized it, I was firing my guns. He ran right into my line of fire. I saw the pilot bail out and the plane burst into flames."

"So the pilot got out alive?" Katie asked.

"Yes he did, but he lost his aircraft. I protected our bombers. We never lost a bomber to the enemy's fighters on long-range escorting duty. In fact, we were so good that we were requested to escort the bombers to Berlin. The bomber pilots didn't want anyone but us "Red Tails" to escort them."

Marcus gave a puzzled look. "What's a Red Tail?"

Cyrum explained, "That's how the Tuskeegee Airmen were identified. The plane's tails were painted red."

"How many of your friends died" Katie asked.

"A lot. More than I care to talk about."

Alarms suddenly went off everywhere. "It's a fire, run for your lives," Marcus yelled loudly, intending to excite the others while feeling less afraid himself.

A man came running up and yelled, "Fire! Get out of here!" He went into the restroom and Tait heard the echo of "Fire" screaming from within the restroom walls. Then a toilet flushed.

Marcus acquired a confident air. "See? I told you."

"Don't panic," Cyrum calmly advised. "Just walk normally to the closest exit."

John Westcamp, one of Tait's classmates, came running up and said the Hope Diamond had been stolen. "The teachers sent us to find everybody. We have to go to the exhibition hall where we came in. We all have to be checked by the police. We are all suspects."

"You mean there is no fire?" Marcus asked.

"It's not a fire. The Hope Diamond was stolen. It's a burglar alarm," corrected John. "Someone shoved a black cloth bag over the guard's head and held him at gun point."

"Wow! This is neat," Tait explained. "We are here when the Hope Diamond is stolen."

The kids were all lined up along the entrance side wall. Many Dayton police officers had come into the building. Tait overheard a detective talking to the museum curator.

"It was the only time all day no one was in the exhibition room, except Walker," the curator explained. "Walker was sitting with his back toward the north entrance."

"So the thief entered from the north hall?" the officer clarified.

"Yes. He sneaked up behind Walker, and slipped a bag over his head. Walker was facing the diamond exhibit."

" Why was he sitting?"
"The guards were given permission to sit. They were taking one-hour shifts. An hour standing in one spot is hard on the legs," explained the man.

"How many school children are in here?" the detective asked

"Two hundred and fifty-three," the curator replied.

"How many adults?"

"Sixty-six including 23 museum personnel," he answered. "The burglar alarms went off automatically when the diamond was removed from the case."

"All right, all right," the detective said and walked over to another officer.

"All outside doors were guarded. The thief has to be in the building," the detective said to the other officer. "Search everybody," the detective instructed and turned away.

"Even the kids?" the officer asked with a surprised look.

"Especially, the kids," he muttered with contempt.

The boys were taken, one at a time into a room and the girls were taken to another. They were stripped down to their underwear and their clothes were searched. Their shoes were checked, their pant pockets, everything.

Once released and outside, the kids ran like galloping horses to the school bus.

Tait stood observing each person in line. The adults were lined up, single file, and taken to another room one by one. Tait spotted Cyrum in line. He was the only black person. Cyrum was looking the room over when he noticed Tait looking at him so he waved him over. Tait quickly checked to see if the teachers were looking and they were not. They were all busy attending to other kid's needs so Tait cut rank, walked slowly over to Cyrum and hid between him and the wall.

"Did you recognize the guy who yelled "fire" back there by the restrooms?" Cyrum asked.

"No," Tait answered. "Who is he?"

"The bum that tried to cut your throat yesterday," Cyrum said matter of factly. "Take another look. He is over there being questioned by the guard now. He is about ready to go into the examination room."

Tait stared for a moment in total concentration at the man Cyrum pointed out. Tait could only see the man's back and was having trouble identifying him. The man had on business like clothes and new black leather dress shoes. His hair cut looked fresh. Nothing similiar to the appearance of the bum except maybe the size of the man.

"Are you sure Cyrum?" Tait questioned. "I don't see any resemblence at all."

Then the man turned around and looked back at the crowd, exposing his clean shaven face. Tait gasped. Tait recognized the sunken sockets of his eyes and the merciless wicked stare. It was the bum. He had shaved his beard, his mustache, and gotten a haircut but the demon behind his eyes was unmistakable. Tait shivered with fright and knew it was undeniably the derelict. Tait noticed the bum's pants were wet in front. The toilet must have flushed water on him, too. Then Tait remembered the man that yelled "fire" and ran into the restroom. It was him. The bum.

"How could he have followed me here?" Tait asked confounded.

"He didn't," Cyrum replied. "He came for some other reason I suspect." Cyrum pulled out something from his back pocket. It was the brochure of the museum he received when he entered the building. He took out a pen and wrote his phone number on it and then handed it to Tait. "Call me tonight. We can talk. I told you this bum was dangerous. He recognized us. He is extremely dangerous now. He is up to something and he knows we know it. Be careful!"

An officer walked up and asked Cyrum where he worked. Cyrum said he was unemployed at the present time. They took Cyrum up front and into the examination room. Tait walked back to his class and got in line. Tait didn't see Cyrum again and wondered about it on the bus ride home.

That evening after supper Tait's dad read the paper aloud from his easy chair. Tait's dad often yelled into the kitchen to inform his wife of the latest news. Tait's mom and his sister Katie spent time cleaning up the dishes after meals. Katie still received an allowance but had to work for it. The Hope Diamond theft was front-page news.

"They still have not found the thief nor the diamond. The museum is closed to the public until further notice," his dad yelled out. "It's just like my son, to be there when the robbery took place. Now I'll never hear the end of this. Tait, I don't want you getting envolved in this. You're always playing detective. Stay away from the museum," he ordered.

Tait wanted to call Cyrum but had to wait for his chance at the phone when no one would overhear his conversation.

"Lord help us," his dad said under his breath, and shook the paper noisily to fold it over to a new page.

The one phone they had was in the kitchen. Tait decided to help with the dishes to speed things up. When everyone was out of the kitchen, he could make his call. His mom was tickled by the fact that her son was so generous. She thought just maybe he was growing up and becoming appreciative of all she had done for him.

Tait's chance came. The kitchen was dark and Tait decided to keep it that way. He left the lights off. Using his flashlight to view the numbers he dialed Cyrum's phone. Listening to each ring gave him a rush of emotion. After the fourth ring he thought maybe Cyrum wasn't home. Maybe the police had him locked up.

"Hello," came the reply.

"Cyrum! You okay," Tait blurted out, not even introducing himself.

"Yeah, I'm alright," he said recognizing Tait's voice. "They gave me a hard time but they had nothing on me. They had to let me go."

"That bum knows where I live," Tait said concerned. "Do you think he's going to try and get me?"

"Don't know. My advice is never to go places alone. This thing will blow over. Don't worry. Bums like him can't stay in one place long. They get antsie."

"Cyrum, I've been thinking. The bum stole the diamond and I know how he did it."

"So you think you figured it out?"

"Yeah, I need you to meet me at the downtown

45

library."

"Okay, when?"

"Saturday morning at 9:00 A.M. Somebody's coming. See you there," Tait said and hung up.

No. 1957

abus Day Celebration, Cooper
, in front of the library, Oct.
1892. Looking west across the
ai and Erie Canal, in the fore-
nd is a canal boat.

ographed by Ed. Curtis.

Chapter 4

Library Clues

Tait heeded Cyrum's advice and brought Katie and Marcus along on his trip to the library. Riding their bicycles up the cement walk to the front door of the library, Tait pointed out Canal Street. "Do you know that the canal went through town right there by the library?"

"You're kidding," Marcus said riding over and taking a closer look at the name on the street sign. "It does say Canal Street."

"See how the street is sunken down deep like that.

They just filled in the canal and made it a street."

"You mean there was a river right over there with boats on it?"

"Yeah, that's what a canal is Marcus. A man-made river."

"Maybe we can find an old picture of it here in the library," Katie suggested.

"I'm not interested in that right now," Tait replied. "I need to find Cyrum."

They walked into the front door of the library, passed the reception desk, and looked around for Cyrum. A librarian came up.

"May I help you with something?" the librarian asked.

"Yes, do you have any old pictures of the canal?" Katie inquired.

"Yes we do. In fact, if you go down to the basement there is a picture hanging on the wall. A canal boat is floating past the library in that picture. The photo was taken in 1892. Things are a little different today. Patterson Boulevard used to be a canal years ago."

"I need a book on sewers," Tait told the lady abruptly.

"Sewers, did you say?" the librarian inquired, a little startled.

"Yes," Tait replied.

"Do you want storm sewers or sanitary sewers?" she asked forcing Tait to a level of detail he didn't know.

"The kind that toilets use," Tait replied.

"You probably mean waste management," she said trying to be helpful. "Doing a research project for school are you?"

Tait just smiled.

The librarian went to the card catalog and wrote down a bunch of numbers. "Just follow me," she said, walking along at a brisk pace. Turning into an aisle of books, she placed her finger on several books and then removed one, and then two more. "Department of Public Works, Sanitary Sewer Systems, Wastewater Treatment," she said out loud. "Here are three books for you to browse through. If you need further assistance just let me know," she said and walked away.

"That was quick," Marcus acknowledged. "It would have taken me all day to find these books."

"That's why they have librarians, Marcus," Katie said smirking. "I'm going to the basement and try to find that photo of the canal next to the library. Bye!"

"I'll go look for Cyrum," Marcus said and wandered off.

"Now is the hard part," Tait thought as he turned the pages of the Wastewater Treatment book. "I wish Cyrum would get here."

The quiet of the library put Tait into a gentle slumber of thought, unconscious of the world around him. An adult starred at him and approached slowly, getting very close and examining the book Tait had open. The foul smell of alcohol and stench of breath broke Tait's attention.

"A sudden interest in sewers, sonny boy!" blurted the man as he leaned on the table.

Tait was petrified. The red veins in the man's eyes and the eyeball's hynotic spell captured Tait so that he couldn't look elsewhere. The bum gave no warning. He was suddenly just there. The bum reached for Tait's shirt and pulled him closer to whisper loudly his threat.

"You can't hide from me kid. I'm going to get you. I can make accidents happen. I told you to stay out of my business," he said as the stink from his breath punctuated the meaning of his words.

Tait saw a black hand gripping the throat of the bum cutting off his words. He choked as he tried to free himself from the grip.

"I can make accidents happen too. You touch this boy and I'll find you. Then I'll make you wish you were never born," Cyrum said as he let the man go.

The bum, in shock, rubbed his throat and staggered to a standing position. "I'll kill you someday," he said backing away and pointing his finger at Cyrum. He departed like an angry wounded animal.

"How did that guy find me?" Tait asked, worried.

"Libraries are famous hangouts for bums," Cyrum replied. "They use the public restrooms and sleep."

"I know how he stole the Hope Diamond."

"Keep talking. I'm interested in hearing this."

"The bum flushed the diamond down the toilet."

Cyrum just stood there thinking.

"His pants were wet like mine. The toilet splashed on him."

"So?"

"He came running up to us yelling fire and then ran into the restroom and yelled fire. Then I heard a toilet flush."

"So?"

"There wasn't anyone in the restroom but him. I was just in there. He ran in, flushed the toilet and ran right back out. He didn't have time to use the toilet."

"The alarms had just gone off so the timing is right," agreed Cyrum. "He obviously lied. There was no fire."

"That's why I asked you to come to the library. We need to figure out where the toilet water goes."

"I saw the photo of the library with the canal boat in it," Katie said out of breath after running up the steps from the basement. "It's pretty neat. Come and see it."

"Not right now. I'm studying sewers," Tait said,

begging off.

Tait turned the pages of the books fast, trying to locate a brief description of how the sanitary sewer system worked.

"It's got to be in here someplace," Tait said frustrated.

"Here," Cyrum said taking the book. "Let me help you."

He turned to the index and read to himself as he checked out the pages. "Here, on page 133 there is a picture of a treatment plant and a lift station," Cyrum said.

Cyrum read, "Most mainline sanitary sewers are designed to maintain an average flow rate between 5 to 10 feet per second, or 5 miles per hour."

Tait thought for a minute and said out loud, "If the sewage Treatment Plant is 10 miles away, it will take 2 hours for the Hope Diamond to get there."

"But what if the diamond got caught up in the sludge or toilet paper somewhere?" Katie interjected.

"Good point. I don't know."

"Listen to this," Cyrum said and began to read

again.

"Most solids in the sewer flow unobstructed all the way to the sewage treatment plant. Many city sewer systems install a series of lift stations. Lift stations have large pumps that pick up the sewage, elevate it higher, and allow it to run down the pipe again. Using lift stations, sewage can be transported many miles."

"What do you think we ought to do?" asked Tait.

"I think I need to go to the Dayton sewer treatment plant. I need to see for myself how these Dayton sewers work. According to this book, sewage treatment plants have big scalping screens that catch solids. I need to see one."

"Can I come?" Tait asked.

"I'll have to call and check when they have public tours of the treatment plant. I might as well go and find out now." Cyrum got up from the table.

"So there you are!" Marcus said as he walked up to Cyrum. "I've been looking all over for you."

"Why don't you kids go home? When I find the times for the tours I'll call you," Cyrum said. He waved goodbye and walked off.

"Why does he want us to go home?" Marcus asked Tait.

"Because the bum just tried to choke me. He promised that he was going to get me. Cyrum chased him away."

Just then, they noticed a kid in a special library station with headphones singing along with the music he was playing on a phonograph. Unaware anyone was watching him or could hear his music, he gestured and danced from side to side in his chair.

"OH! Hot diggity, dog ziggity boom, what'cha do to me. It's so new to me. What'cha do to me. ..." the kid was disturbing everyone around him. When he got to the part where he said, "Never dreamed anybody could kiss thata way," Tait and Marcus burst out laughing uncontrollably.

The librarian came over and tapped the kid on the shoulder and he jumped, practically falling out of his chair. His face turned red when he realized the whole place was looking at him. Embarrassed, he got up and left.

Rags, the local street bum in his mid-forties, had been sleeping face down on a book at the next table over. When he lifted his head his cheek was red and sleep lines creased his face, revealing he had been there a long time.

The man had wrapped an old tattered coat around himself. His shirt was ripped under the arm pits. His blue jeans were torn at the knees and his rear was so worn that small holes revealed the inside of his back pockets. His naturally brown hair hung below his shoulders, uncombed with curls knotted, making him look like a wild man. His hair was soiled from sleeping on the ground, probably by the river. He was harmless and everybody knew it. He strolled the city streets freely, annoying people for coins now and then. On cold days he slept in the library.

Now that the loud music had ended and the kids stopped laughing he lumbered over to Tait's study table and looked around. He bent over and whispered to Tait.

"What's going on?"

"Nothing," Tait said. "Some kid was just singing to music and disturbing everybody."

"I mean with you and that black man," he said, divulging the fact he had been faking sleep. He had been alert and observing Tait for awhile. The bum sat down, unwelcomed.

"He was just helping us with our homework," Tait said figuring it wasn't a lie. It was detective homework.

"You wouldn't happen to have a couple of quarters on you would you?" Rags begged in a tender voice.

"No," Tait replied not even looking up from his book.

"A guy's got to eat. Do you have a dime?"

"I'm plum out of money," Tait said unsympathetically.

Katie reached over and handed Rags a quarter.

"Thanks young lady. You're a sweetheart," he said with a great big grin.

"What are you going to do with it?" Marcus asked. "Buy liquor?"

"Heck no. I'm not a drunk. I'm just down on my luck. I can buy a big deli sandwich down at Midnight Market on Third and Linden. The local market is a good meeting place. I run into most of my friends at one time or another there."

"You got friends," Marcus said sarcastically.

"Yes, buddy boy. I got lots of them. They're all street people down on their luck, but we help each other. The market is where we meet and pass along the latest news."

"What news? What do you guys know?" Marcus questioned.

"There is a hum around town about who has the Hope Diamond. The newspapers don't give you information like that. No sir."

"The Hope Diamond. You know who has it?" Tait asked.

"Well not exactly."

"That figures. Not exactly means he doesn't know," Marcus chimed in.

"I know more than you think," Rags replied with pride. "Duck Lady's been involved with trying to pawn the thing off. That's the latest word," he said matter of factly, not giving any indication of bragging.

"Duck Lady. Who is that?" Katie asked inquisitively.

"I thought everyone knew Duck Lady. She goes quack quack all over town. Never talks to anyone. Just quacks."

"I've seen her before," Tait said. "I saw her in front of Rike's department store. She waddles like a duck and quacks."

"That's her. She has walked the city streets for years. She is talking now. To her friends that is. She is not as dumb as you think."

"Well, how did she get the Hope Diamond?" Tait asked.

"I don't know. You're going to have to ask her."

"How do I find her?" Tait asked.

"Go to the Midnight Market on Third street. She goes there. Best deli sandwiches in town and the best price. You will know her by her quack."

"When will she be there? We can't just wait there all day," Marcus said.

"Lunch, wise guy. When else?"

"So when is lunch?" Marcus asked again.

"When ever you get there," Rags retorted.

"That helps a lot," Marcus said a bit angrily.

"Obviously sometime around noon," Tait said to Marcus.

"So are you going to be there, Rags?" Katie asked.

"Not today. I'm going to eat at Wympee's Restaurant today."

Tait looked at his watch. "We have plenty of time to get to the Midnight Market. Let's go now."

"The bum might be outside waiting for us. I'm going to check," Marcus said and took off. Marcus ran back and shouted that he spotted the bum reading a newspaper over by the front door."

"You mean he is still here?" Tait said frantically.

"Yes!"

Tait looked at Rags and asked, "Do you know who that bum reading the newspaper is?"

"Probably, I know most of the street people in town."

"Tell us his name," Tait asked.

They all got up and stood as a group in the front lobby gazing at the man sitting at the reading table, hiding behind a newspaper.

When Rags got a glimpse of his face he smiled and said, "That's Jerry. He hops on trains and travels the country following warm weather usually. Strange he is still in town."

"Thanks," Tait said and gathered Marcus and Katie to his side. Whispering to them in a football like huddle, he layed out his plans. "We will walk slowly to the door and then run to our bikes. We can reach the Midnight Market by noon in time for lunch. I can hardly wait to meet Duck Lady."

The plan worked. They were on their bikes rolling along. Tait felt his leg muscles pushing the bicycles peddles hard, moving him swiflly away from the library. He looked back and saw Jerry, the bum, swing the front doors of the library open and watch them cycle away.

Chapter 5

Street People Talk

The mural on the side of the building made the
Midnight Market easy to spot. The mural depicted people
selling groceries at a farmers market. Since Katie's
bicycle was a smaller "girl's bike", she had to peddle
faster to keep up with Tait, who slowed down so they
could ride side by side and talk. Marcus was his jolly self
and bragged how they got away from that sleezy bum,
Jerry.

The store we are looking for is just up ahead on the

corner," Tait shouted. "Be careful. I see a couple of dogs."

The kids leaned their bicycles against the brick wall of the grocery store and petted the dogs. The Airedale wagged his tail and body frantically, stood on his hind legs and licked Tait in the face.

"Down boy, down boy," Tait kept saying as he backed away from the mutt. The other little dog just sniffed at Marcus' leg.

"That little dog is a Springer Spaniel," Katie said. "They're real friendly dogs. They make good pets."

"Get off of me you dumb dog," Tait said pushing the Airedale away.

Katie started to walk to the front of the grocery store so Tait followed as the dogs ran around in circles following.

"We must be early for lunch," Tait remarked. "There are no people around here anywhere."

Traffic was busy on Third Street. Cars and trucks went by, fast and noisy. A yellow trolley bus slowed down in front of them as if to stop. Tait realized they were under a bus stop sign, and waved the bus on. The sky was gray and overcast. There was a mist in the air with a slight breeze. All three kids were shivering.

"Maybe the street people are inside the store because of the cold," Katie suggested.

"Yeah, let's go in and look around and stay warm," Marcus urged.

"We should have worn warmer cloths. I'm freezing," Tait said pulling on the grocery store door.

Two men were standing next to the front door conversing about politics with the owner who was behind the check-out counter managing the cash register. The owner smiled and nodded to the kids as they entered, all the while listening to the political views of the men.

"This place must be a hundred years old," Tait said kicking a piece of tile to the edge of the aisle. Square tiles with faded blue colors covered the floor and some were missing. The floor was uneven as if an earthquake had rolled the floor into stationary waves. The aisle-ways were narrow with only enough room for one grocery cart. A person could not stand still without blocking the path of another shopper.

"Uh-oh," said Katie panicking, as she kicked a box of cereal that was on the floor with the lid open, spilling out a pile of flakes. "I hope they don't think I did this."

The owner came over and looked at Tait. "I didn't do this," Tait said emphatically.

"I know. I just went and got this broom and dustpan to clean it up. A customer did it with his cart. Happens all the time. What is your name?"

"Tait," he said.

"I'm Katie," Katie interjected.

The owner bent over and placed the dustpan on the floor and looked up at Marcus, "And you sir, what is your name?"

Marcus smirked at the reference that he was a sir and spoke up, "My name is Marcus."

"Glad to meet you. I'm Joe. I own this place. Go ahead and look around. I have pretty good prices," he said and knelt on the floor to scoop up the scattered cereal.

Tait and Katie went on to the rear of the store

where the meat counter displayed freshly cut deli meats. No one was behind the counter so they just looked for awhile at all the different kinds of meats and cheeses. Then Joe appeared behind the counter and spoke up. "May I help you kids with something?"

"Are you the butcher, too?" Katie asked.

"I do it all in this store. I'm a Jack of all trades I guess," he said happily.

"Yes, I would like a sandwich," Tait said, looking the selection over.

"Why are you buying a sandwich?" Katie asked puzzled, knowing Mom had the same stuff at home for free.

"Because I'm hungry," Tait said to Katie, a little angrily. He was trying to play it cool, acting like a shopper, and Katie was ignorant of his plan. "We have to stay in the store for awhile and I don't want him kicking us out," he said in a whisper. "Maybe Duck Lady will come in."

"I'll take a sandwich too," she said to Joe. "I want two thin slices of ham with mayonnaise, lettuce and cheese. No pickle."

"Make my sandwich the same way," Tait said, acknowledging Katie had ordered a good sandwich. Do you have potato chips?"

"Yes, right over there," he said pointing.

"Are you paying for your own sandwich?" Tait asked.

"No, you are. I'm not spending my allowance money on a sandwich. You have the paper route and can afford to pay for both of us."

"I was afraid of that," Tait said disgruntled.

"Could you loan me some money Tait? I don't have enough," Marcus begged.

Tait begrudingly gave Marcus a buck knowing he would never get it back. The kids meandered up and down the aisles for about ten minutes eating their sandwiches and chips when Tait spotted a coke machine tucked along the office wall by the back door. On the side of the red machine was written 5 cents in white letters. Tait put a nickel in the machine. He snapped the cap off with the bottle opener embedded in the pop machine, and gave the soda to Katie. Before he could insert a second nickel into the machine for another pop, a man dressed like an automobile mechanic shoved his nickel into the slot. No pop came out. He began banging his greasy fist against the machine.

"This darn machine stole my nickel," he said kicking the bottom. He then put his shoulder against the side of the coke machine and pushed. The whole machine wobbled back and forth. "Go ahead kid, try your luck."

Tait was afraid not to put in his nickel since the man was so upset. The nickel tinkled down the chamber starting a clunking noise and ending with a bang. The coke lay at the bottom of the opening and Tait grabbed it.

"Kids have all the luck. I'll try one more nickel and I better get my coke this time," the man ranted as he plunked his nickel into the machine. A coke plopped out. He grabbed it, forced it against the bottle opener and yanked the cap off, took a quick drink, and walked away without saying a word.

Tait could hear Joe talking to the man. "Frank, don't break my machine for gosh sakes. I'll give you your nickel back."

Joe came back and to their surprise, called the kids by their names. "Tait, are you finding everything you're looking for?" he asked with a smile.

"Yes, thank you," Tait replied. "Do you know you have wild dogs outside?" Tait informed him, trying to think of something intelligent to say.

"They are all friendly neighborhood dogs. They wouldn't hurt anyone." "It's the street people we have to run off. They buy their sandwiches and pint size wines, sit out back and make a nuisance of themselves."

"I didn't see any street people outside," Tait said acting innocent.

"Oh, they will be here, especially on a cold day like today. They come inside to get warm and then go back outside again. Every Saturday you will see two or three of them hanging around outback."

"So what's wrong with that?"

"The neighbors don't like the bums hanging around. Our customers don't like it either. Bums congregate by the entrance asking for money."

"Like asking for a quarter," Katie said knowing the experience.

"Yeah, you got that right."

"We deal with our customers on a personal level. I know most of them by name. They stop coming here if the street people hang around outside pestering them. So we run them off when they get to be a nuisance. The city mayor lives two doors down you know."

"Really," Tait said surprised.

"Yeah, that's why we get good cooperation from the police when we need it. I've seen people pushing buggies down the alleys at 5:00A.M. in the morning. Garbage picking, they collect pop bottles and stuff like that."

A grungy old codger came into the store and ordered a baloney sandwich. He reached into the freezer and pulled out a beer. He opened the beer and began drinking out of it before he paid for it.

"Don't go milling around outside scaring away my customers," Joe said. "Go back downtown to the park."

"These people sure know where to find the

bargains," Katie said amazed.

Tait noticed a short woman about as tall as Katie standing perfectly still. She then started walking in a wobbling fashion. She had bowed legs and wore tennis shoes. She took a few small steps and then stopped again, and looked around. She was about sixty, Tait guessed. She had a little Dachshund in her arms. She gazed at Tait and then came over.

"Hey sonny! Do you have a quarter?" she asked. "I need a bone for my dog."

"No, I don't have an extra quarter."

She bent over to let her dog smell Tait's arm. "Rosy won't bite you. Will you Rosy? Rosy needs a quarter."

The dog bit Tait on the arm getting a mouth full of jacket.

"Well, that's the first time Rosy has ever bitten anyone. I'm so sorry. Are you all right?"

Tait rubbed his arm and said, "Yes, I'm all right."

"You should have been more friendly toward my dog. She sensed your fear and rejection," the lady said as

71

she walked off.

"Boy can you beat that. The lady's dog bites me and she says it's my fault. I hate people like that."

"So the dog bit you, huh?" Joe asked. "Are you hurt bad?"

"No, the bite didn't break the skin. Luckily I had a coat on."

"These street people can be a pain. If she causes you any more trouble, you let me know," he said.

The Airedale sneaked into the store and came up and sniffed on Tait's leg.

"These darn dogs around here get fed better than we do," Joe remarked. "Come here you little mutt," he said as the dog ran around the corner of the next aisle.

"I'll get him for you," yelled Marcus and chased after the dog.

"Have you ever seen Duck Lady?" Tait asked.

"Oh yeah. Now there is a wacko for you. Most everyone who goes downtown Dayton knows her. She is famous in a way. You'll know her if you see her," said Joe, waddling in place and going quack, quack. The immitation drew laughter from Tait. "She hangs out downtown mostly among the masses of people who occupy the sidewalks during rush hour. She loves being in a crowd. Crazy, huh?"

"Sounds a little crazy," Tait agreed.

"She hurries herself through the crowds to some unknown destination every day like she has important business to take care of. People just look at her and wag their heads. At the crosswalks she quacks like a hurt duck until the walk sign turns green and then she waddles across the street. She's harmless. The city workers, businessmen, and shoppers all talk about her since she is such an oddity. You can see fingers pointing from the big windows of the city buses as they go by her, as if she is a tourist attraction."

"Why did she go crazy, I wonder?" Katie asked.

"Do you want me to tell you a secret?" Joe said, lowering his voice.

"Sure," Katie replied.

He leaned over the top of Tait and whispered in her ear. "She is the daughter of one of the wealthiest families

73

in town. No kidding, so help me God," Joe said and stood up straight like a congressman.

"She is what you call a lost sheep. Not many people know that. A few relatives know but that's all. It is a very well-kept secret."

"How do you know it then?" Tait asked.

"I'm one of the few people she talks to. She visits her sister at Christmas time and whenever she needs money."

"The gossip around town is that she is trying to sell the Hope Diamond. You would think she would try to sell it to one of her rich relatives if she had it," Joe said. "That would make sense."

Just then a lady in a long black coat and a big brimmed hat came into the grocery. She was carrying a small black purse and a shopping bag. Her black shoes had large flat heels. She scuffled along as she walked the aisle to the Coke machine. The Airedale ran over to her and wagged its tail and smelled her. "Quack, quack," she replied to the dog, as she scooted along.

"There she is," hollered Joe, pointing.

"Call her over here so we can talk to her," Tait begged.

"Can't do that."

"Why not?"

"She has to warm up to you even if you're a friend. You always start over from scratch. She doesn't trust anybody."

"I've got to catch that dog," he said as he jogged after it, yelling for Marcus to go the opposite way so they could corner it.

Tait noticed a gumball machine behind the potato chip stand close to the deli. Tait decided to put in a penny while keeping an eye on Duck Lady. He could see prizes along with all the gum through the round glass ball. One neat prize was a miniature silver cigarette lighter. The machine returned a round piece of gum that he began chewing vigorously, but none of the neat prizes came down the shute with the gumball.

A big fat hand slapped down on top the machine. Tait looked up and gasped.

"Boys can't be too careful these days where they

hang out. Some get hurt being in the wrong place at the wrong time," said Jerry, the bum. "You thought you got rid of me in the library, didn't you?"

Tait was speechless. Katie was horrified. Marcus was screaming out that he had caught the dog.

Jerry picked up the gum machine, iron stand and all. He wobbled it around until the prize he wanted fell into the opening. He set it back on the floor and put in his penny. Out came a tiny silver cigarette lighter. He flicked the lighter producing a small flame. He lit a cigarette and then went over and leaned against the deli counter looking over the meats. Duck Lady quacked as she came up behind the man, and then nudged her way beside him. Joe appeared.

"I'll take a ham sandwich please," she said ordering ahead of Jerry. "Mustard only on rye bread."

As soon as she got her sandwich she went to the check-out counter and quacked to let Joe know she wanted to leave immediately. "Just a minute, Jerry," Joe said. "Let me take care of Margaret. She seems to be in a hurry today."

Katie whispered to Tait and said, "Duck Lady's name must be Margaret."

Duck Lady opened the door to leave and Marcus, clinging to the Airedale, bumped her sideways.

"Sorry," Marcus quipped, and dropped the scrambling dog out the door.

Duck Lady went out, followed by Tait pushing Marcus through the door. With Katie trailing behind they went to their bicycles and sat on them pretending to be leaving. A man sitting in an expensive car parked along the curb waved his arms out the window and yelled, "Margaret." Duck Lady went over. They talked. The man was dressed in a suit like a businessman. He wore a top hat with a brim. A large rectangular diamond ring was on his left hand as it rested on the car door.

"I hear you have something for sale," the man said. She spoke softly in the man's ear. He smiled. Tait heard only a few words of the conversation: "…railroad bridge over by DP&L…sewage plant…tomorrow morning…"

"Tait!" Marcus warned. "Jerry is coming."

Duck Lady walked away eating her sandwich, and

strolled to the bus stop.

Suddenly Jerry paused, and changed his direction to that of the luxury automobile. He got in. The car moved out into traffic and went its way.

Tait was puzzled that Jerry didn't beat them up until he turned to look for Duck Lady at the bus stop and saw a man standing there talking with her. He was wearing the infamous tin can man suit.

"Cyrum," he said gleefully. "I can't believe you're here." Tait gazed at the man stunned. "You're not Cyrum?"

"No, Cyrum is a friend of mine. I'm Dennis Tucker," he said.

"You're the real Tin Can Man!" Katie said terror-stricken.

Now don't be freightened. I won't hurt you," he said as he stooped to listen to Duck Lady speak into his ear as she tugged on his arm.

"No," he said to Duck Lady and then addressed the children. "Cyrum is quite a fellow. Brave, honest and humble," Dennis said proudly. "Met him at church. He walked in my shoes for a day. Wore my clothes and pushed my cart. Why, the man shook the hand of President Harry Truman and he is nice enough to help me."

Tait noticed that Duck Lady just sat her empty coke bottle down on the sidewalk next to the light pole on which the bus stop sign hung. She quacked a couple of times and then put one foot into the street. She turned and looked for the bus among the traffic.

The bus came barreling toward the curb and stopped abruptly. Duck Lady got on. Tait could barely see Duck Lady through the bus window as it left the stop. Her head was down low so only her hat was visible.

"Jerry was about to get us," Katie said making Dennis aware of the crisis.

"Cyrum told me to keep an eye out for you kids."

"Duck Lady is selling the Hope Diamond. They guy buying it just left in his car," Tait explained. "We need to tell Cyrum. They are meeting sometime tomorrow at some railroad bridge by a water falls."

"There is only one bridge like that around here,"

Dennis said. "I fish there. In fact, I'll have Cyrum fish there tomorrow morning with me. Why don't you meet us there? Bring your fishing gear, and I'll show you how to catch fish."

"Okay!" agreed Tait. "We'll come right after we deliver Sunday papers.

"I can pack sandwiches and pop and get things ready," Katie added.

"Good idea. Pack the binoculars, too."

"Now that we have a plan why don't you kids jump into my cart and I'll push you home," Dennis said with a smile. "I'll give you protection. Nobody messes with me."

Off they went, bicycles and all, in the huge cart as Tin Can Man pushed the buggy down the alley. Dennis kept their attention with one of Cyrum's war exploits over enemy territory. This time Cyrum's aircraft was crippled from machine gun fire and about to go down.

"Cyrum, a prisoner of war?" went through Tait's mind

Chapter 6

The Bridge

That night Tait, Katie, and Marcus talked about Cyrum's incredible war stories and agreed it would be fun to be a pilot. They also firmed up their fishing plans and schemed of methods to sneak up on the criminals.

"I think we ought to split up, fish separately and keep our ears and eyes open," Tait suggested. "We can cover more area that way."

"I disagree," Marcus argued. "We better stick together for protection."

No one agreed on anything that night. Tait's family

was asleep when he got out of bed. The weather had changed from 38°, rainy and cold, to 58°, and dry. The expected high was to be 76°, and sunny. Dayton, Ohio weather was like that. Some people called the warm weather, after the first cold and frost of autumn, Indian summer.

Tait quickly delivered his paper route and when he walked into his house Katie was ready. She was true to her word. She had six peanut butter and jelly sandwiches, apples, gum, and Snickers candy bars packed for the trip. Three cokes were also included. Marcus arrived delighted to see lunch packed. He began fingering the candy bars.

"You can't eat anything until we get there," Katie said, making it a rule.

"You got your fishing gear, Marcus?" Tait asked.

"Yep," he said, patting his jeans front pocket. "I've got a knife, and my hooks and sinkers are in this little plastic box." Marcus showed them.

They all three carried their fishing poles across their handlebars.

"What about bait?" Marcus asked.

"Dough balls," Tait said holding up a loaf of bread.

When they got to the Stuart Street Bridge they stopped to look at the river.

"We're here. Where do we go next?" asked Katie.

"We go up river to the railroad bridge. It's big with iron works on top. It's easy to spot," Marcus said.

"I think we go down river," Tait said, disagreeing. "I know there is a flat railroad bridge next to a waterfall."

"Duck Lady walks around downtown. There is an old steel truss bridge downtown, right where she would normally be walking," Marcus argued.

"Maybe you're right," Tait conceded. "Let's go check it out."

They rode their bikes down along the river and stopped right under the bridge.

"There is nobody around here," Katie said.

"I wonder on which side of the bridge they plan to meet," Marcus said.

"This is not a good meeting place. You can't get to either side of the tracks without going onto private property," Tait said, questioning the correctness of their choice.

"Look! 'No Trespassing' signs," Katie said, finding an old sign whose painted letters were mostly gone.

"I think we are at the wrong bridge," Tait said.

"Didn't you hear the man in the car say the bridge next to DP&L?" Katie asked.

"Yes, you're right. It is the other bridge. I should not have listened to Marcus. Now we might miss the meeting."

They turned their bikes around and headed down river. Marcus rode ahead fast, laughing as if he were somehow a better biker than they were. Katie tried to keep up with Marcus but couldn't. Tait was last as he rode steady but sulking at his failure to go with his own instincts. He let Marcus bully him again into doing the wrong thing.

When they saw the Carillon Bells ahead they got excited. "The falls are below the train bridge up another half mile," Tait explained. We will stop there and make camp."

The roar of the water was thrilling and the smell of the dead fish established the place as a fishing site. They rode effortlessly, even though they had biked almost ten miles.

A black man was sitting above the falls with his feet up against the protective fence. He was fishing the best spot and using two poles. Both were cast below the falls where the bait freely floated downstream. His hat was full of lures and hooks. His jacket was multi-colored with leather sleeves. His tackle box was full of fishing equipment, and a fishing net rested against the fence. He never noticed the kids until they were upon him.

It was Tait who first recognized the man and turned to Marcus saying, "It's Cyrum."

"Did you catch any fish?" Marcus yelled as he stepped on his brakes and slid down the asphalt hill slanting his bike sideways into a screeching halt.

"Go down to the shore line and pull up that stringer," he said with a smile.

Marcus ran down and pulled up his stringer,

showing off six lively fish.

"Wow, what kind are they?" Marcus asked.

"Two blue gills, three cat fish, and a sucker fish," Cyrum answered. "People say there are bass in here but I never caught one."

"There are carp in here also," Tait said.

"Yeah, there are plenty of carp in here. They have a mud vein you know. Once you get the mud vein out you can eat them," said Cyrum adding a little helpful information.

"Where is Tin Can Man?" Tait asked.

"He couldn't make it but told me about our meeting."

"Look at all those ducks over there," Katie pointed out.

"Some of those are Canada geese," amended Cyrum. "You see a lot of them around here. Blue Heron walk the shoreline also. I've even seen a pair of white swan down by the beaver dam."

"Beaver dam," whooped Marcus excited about the prospect of locating it.

"The dam is way down river," Cyrum said chuckling at the vivacious curiosity of the children. "You can't catch fish unless your line is in the water."

Marcus threw his line back into the water and asked, "What kind of bait are you using?"

"Red worms. Want some?"

"Yeah," Marcus said loudly. "Give me two. The more meat on the hook the better."

Katie chose to use the red worms too but asked Cyrum to put her worm on the hook. About the time they got their poles in the water, Marcus decided he was hungry.

"You get only one Snickers, Marcus," Katie said scolding him when she saw he had two.

"I know. I'm just looking to see what else is in the bag," he said while unloading all the goodies.

Tait tried to use his bread for bait to catch a carp but it kept falling off.

"Bread doesn't work that well," Cyrum stated. "Do you want to use some of my bait?"

"Sure, thanks," Tait answered. Cyrum gave him

some dough balls he had made from corn flakes.

"I put some special smells on these dough balls to attract the fish," he said. Tait put his nose to the dough ball and gagged.

"Why would a fish eat this stinky thing?" he asked.

"It smells good to a fish. Go ahead. Throw your line out there and try your luck. A big carp is waiting for breakfast."

Tait threw his line into the water and impatiently reeled it in again. "Leave your bait in the water," Cyrum suggested. "The fish will swim around and find it. The smell will attract them. Get a twig and let your pole rest. That's how you fish for carp."

"This is kind of boring," Tait said.

"If you want a lot of action go fly fishing. You cast out and reel in the fly constantly. Bass like to see the fly move. You need a special rod and reel. The water is too muddy here. Fly fishing is fun."

"I think I'll switch to red worms," Tait said bored. "I can cast more." He began reeling in his line until it got stuck.

"Shoot! I'm snagged. I think I'm hooked on a small log," Tait figured. He kept pulling the object closer to shore tugging it along.

"That log of yours has fins," Marcus said laughing. "You got a fish."

Tait held up his pole dangling the fish in the air. "This fish didn't fight. It just laid in the water like a log. I didn't even know I had a fish."

"Carp are like that. They are not a game fish. They don't struggle," Cyrum explained.

Tait was so agitated at the lack of excitement at catching his carp that he picked it up over his head and threw the fish back into the river leaving the hook in its mouth. This time he reeled it in like it was the first time he hooked it. He screamed and hollered, giving everyone a real show.

Marcus could not let Tait outshine him, so he too screamed and hollered as he reeled something in. It turned out to be an old gym shoe.

"Fishing is fun," Katie told Cyrum. "I never thought it would be."

"Yes, fishing is fun. I like flying better. I remember a nice day like this when I was flying high behind a group of bombers. I was giving them protection you know. I noticed German planes flying above us like a flock of birds. They dived at the bombers. I chased the whole group of them. I shot down one fighter and watched his airplane fall apart. Then I realized I had a German fighter trying to gun me down. I rolled over and down so that I turned back the other way. I got behind him and he started maneuvering a bit. Then he rolled over and I stayed right with him. He looked back and saw me on his tail. The dogfight lasted for a couple of minutes and then I lost him."

Cyrum was interrupted when Tait yelled out. "Look over there on the bridge. It looks like Duck Lady walking across to our side. Give me the binoculars."

"Is it Duck Lady?" Katie asked impatiently.

"It's her all right. She is dressed in black and waddling like a duck."

"Let me see," insisted Marcus. "Why does she wear black all the time?"

"Street people wear black because it makes them invisible," Cyrum said.

"Invisible! How's that?" Katie asked.

"In the dark of the night a person in black can hardly be seen. They can hide in doorways or walk the dark streets and not be seen wearing black."

"Let's get closer," Tait insisted.

They dropped their fishing poles and ran under the bridge. They were huddled together looking up between the gaps of the bridge when Katie said, "We need a plan."

"Give me those binoculars," Tait demanded of Katie. "I see two men at the far end of the bridge."

"I saw a car parked up there by the tracks," Katie informed them.

"Katie and I will climb up closer to the car and keep our ears open. Marcus, keep your eye on Duck Lady from down here with these binoculars.

Climbing up the grassy bank was difficult. The incline was steep and slippery. They both clawed their way to the top, often sliding down a little on their bellies. They got their coats dirty but they made it. They saw

Duck Lady approach the car. They hid behind the huge boulders that formed the base of the bridge and listened. The driver-side window opened and a hand rested on the door.

"Look, Katie," Tait said. "The rectangular diamond ring on the man's finger. Look familiar?"

Duck Lady received something from the man in the car. Words were spoken but the kids couldn't hear anything. The man's hand made motions in the air giving directions. Duck Lady backed away from the car and the window shut. The car slowly moved away and was gone. Duck Lady started back across the bridge. Tait and Katie stayed out of sight until she had passed them. She waddled her tail as she walked alone along the tracks back to her accomplice.

"I saw what she was carrying," Tait said. "It looked like a hacksaw."

"It was a lot smaller than Dad's." Katie observed.

Tait waved for Marcus to come up. Once Duck Lady had crossed the bridge and was out of sight the three of them began crossing the bridge following her tracks.

They got to the other side and heard voices. They laid down on their stomachs between the cold rails of the tracks.

"Keep an eye out for trains. They can sneak up on you," Tait cautioned.

"Be careful not to break the blade," they overheard Duck Lady say to the man talking to her.

"I'll cut the pendant diamonds out of the settings as proof I have the Hope Diamond but next time I want some money," the man said.

"He said to meet at the Carillon Bells next Saturday at noon. Bring the thirteen white diamonds. If he likes what he sees he will give you ten thousand dollars and set up the next meeting to buy the Hope Diamond."

The man went to the sewer plant and Duck Lady walked toward downtown.

The kids went back over the railroad bridge and discussed what they heard with Cyrum.

"I got the license plate number," Tait informed Cyrum.

"Good work," Cyrum said as he cast his line one

more time into the water. We need to get the name of that guy in the car. He's the one buying the diamond."

"These crooks need to be caught before they hurt somebody," Tait said with a sense of purpose in his voice.

"We will all be famous," Marcus stated gleefully.

"Oh, that's incentive," Cyrum said coughing up a laugh.

"Anybody can be famous, even a crook," Cyrum said. "You want to live an honorable life. That's what counts. When is this meeting again?"

"Next Saturday at the Carillon Bells," Tait answered.

"They are going to exchange money for the pendant of white diamonds that surround the Hope Diamond."

"Tait," Cyrum said. "You and I have to visit the sewer plant. We need to figure out how they got the diamond after it went down the toilet. The tour this month is Tuesday at 6:30 P.M. I'll meet you in the parking lot of the sewer plant."

Chapter 7

The Pump Station

Tait got to the sewer plant early. He parked his bicycle, sat down on a cement parking block, and waited for Cyrum. A car drove into the lot and parked. The two women in the car just sat talking. Another car came in slowly. The driver looked at Tait sitting there and parked. An older gentleman got out and went into the building. A pickup truck pulled into the lot and two young men got out. They walked together, chatting as they went toward the front door. Tait could easily hear what they were saying.

"You sure can smell this place," the one man said.

"That smell is money. I got the contract to drain the lagoon and clean it out. You should have smelled this place before I did that."

Tait was happy to see Cyrum arrive. They walked together into the building. There was a meeting room past the guard's office to the right, and the people taking the tour were congregating there. A very talkative and confident woman arrived. She was an environmental scientist, and was giving the tour. Stout and in her forties, she walked energetically among the visitors, laughing at their comments about the smell.

"We are not here to make money," she said giggling. "We are not a business. We are a city service. If you think the smell is bad now you should have been here a few years ago. The odors on the river were bad enough to kill a horse. We fixed that."

"How did you fix it?" a gentleman asked.

"Water carried through storm sewers is discharged

into the rivers untreated. We informed the public not to throw chemicals down storm sewers. It pollutes the water. The fish die and the river stinks. We also made businesses that dumped raw sewage into our system pay big fines. Let's take a walk outside and I'll show you around."

The lady pointed to equipment that looked like space age technology and said, "No, that's not the next Sputnik," she said laughing. "It's used to remove and purify water."

"Where does toilet water go," Tait asked.

"There are hundreds of miles of wastewater sewer lines that flow from your house to the pipes along the roads throughout the city. There are pumping stations along the way. It all comes here to the treatment plant. Does that answer your question?" she asked.

"So toilet water pipes and the sewers in the street are different?" Tait asked.

"That's right. The storm sewers in the street go directly to the river. Toilet water goes through pipes to our treatment plant. Do you understand now," she asked.

"Yes," he said thankfully.

"Organisms are used to naturally treat the water rather than chemicals. Chlorination is used, but then we take the chlorine out of the water again before discharging it into the river.

"Can you walk through the pipes?" Tait interrupted again.

"That's a good one," she said snickering at the thought of walking through passages of gunk. "No one has asked me that question before. The answer is mostly no, unless you're a rat."

Everybody laughed and then she continued her lecture.

"The division operates 24-hours a day. Our mission is to promote health. Are there any more questions?"

The crowd stood silent.

"Let me ask you a question. Why are manhole covers round?"

No one answered. "Stumped you all, huh? Manhole covers are round so that it is impossible for a cover to fall down the manhole. If they were square or rectangular, they could."

"I didn't know that," Tait said to Cyrum, fascinated by the answer.

"The waste water system is gravity powered, but the earth is not level. Gravity cannot do all the work because of hills. In these cases, the sewer system will include a lift station to move the wastewater up over a hill."

"What do lift stations look like?" Cyrum asked.

"They look like concrete silos with a steel plate on top. There is a big pump inside. About once a year we do maintenance on them. You can see a lot of them down along the river. They look like big concrete boxes covered with dirt."

"What if someone lost something down the toilet? Where does it go?" Tait asked.

"All kinds of stuff goes down toilets: lifesaver rolls, pencils, pens, chains, pendants, rings, marbles, house-keys, gold fish."

"My three-year-old son threw a blue toy submarine down our toilet," a man in the crowd said. "My wife was giving him a bath and left the room for a minute. When she came back, the blue submarine was just disappearing in the toilet."

"Yes. You would be surprised what goes down a toilet. The first stage of water treatment involves ponds. The solids, like toys, settle out of the water and sink. The system then collects the solids with a screen for disposal. The screens, made of iron bars, remove large objects, such as sticks and rags. Mechanical rakes remove the material from the surface of the screens. Gold rings, coins and things are collected and sold. They sell it to a scrap dealer. The proceeds are put into a city fund."

"Is there just one guy who collects all this stuff from the screen? I mean he could just pocket some of it," Tait said.

"A number of people are assigned the task of cleaning the screens. It is done during the day with everyone watching. There was a night worker a few years ago who climbed the fence and gathered some of the good stuff for himself. Other workers spotted him, and he was fired."

The tour was over and Tait and Cyrum talked in the parking lot.

"If a city maintenance man set up a screen at a pumping station, he could retrieve the Hope Diamond before it ever got to the sewer plant," Cyrum surmised.

"Yeah," Tait agreed. "That way nobody would notice him. People would think he was just doing his job fixing the pump in the lift station."

"Let's go walk along the river close to the museum and see if we can find a pump station."

Cyrum put Tait's bicycle in the trunk of his car and they rode down to the river road and parked across from the museum. They walked along the river and found a pump station and then noticed another one closer to the museum.

"Do you think we could get the lid off and look inside?" Tait asked.

"I have a tire bar in the car that goes to my jack. Maybe I could use it to pry up the cover."

It worked. They looked into the pit and it was obvious that it had been recently worked on. There were extra pipes lying around and a chicken wire screen.

"Everything is here for someone to divert the water from the main pipe to this runoff," Cyrum said.

"This may be where they snatched the diamond out of the water line. It would only take a few minutes to get here from the museum. This would be a perfect spot if you knew what you were doing," Tait said feeling good that his toilet theory was correct.

Cyrum climbed down into the cement box and fastened the wire screen to the runoff pipe. "This is how they did it. Now this is good evidence."

"The meeting next Saturday at Carillon Bells should prove interesting," Tait said with a smile of certainty.

Cyrum and Tait parted, with their sketchy plan to meet at the Carillon. Tait told Marcus and Katie about the pump station. They were all eager to spy on the criminals.

Going as far as Carillon park required Tait's mother's approval, as did the fishing trip the weekend earlier, so he asked her as she was preparing the evening meal.

"Mom, can I go to Carillon park next Saturday?"

"Again! You just went fishing close by there."

"Yeah, but we didn't go in the park. There is a lot of neat stuff in there." Tait failed to mention the spy activities they were going to engage in.

"It should be very educational," she said and agreed to let them go. "However, I need a favor from you."

"Like what?" Tait asked, not having the foggiest idea what she was about to say.

"I need my wrist watch repaired. I would like you to take it to Oscar Beigel's jewelry store today."

Without hesitation Tait agreed, leaving his mother a little bewildered at his quick response.

This was a stroke of luck, Tait thought to himself. This would give him a chance to talk with the jeweler about the Hope Diamond.

"You will find my watch on top of my dresser in the bedroom," she said. "Why don't you do it now before you forget?" His mother continued making supper while Tait hustled with enthusiasm to the jewelry store.

Chapter 8

The Jeweler

Dressed in his best suit, Mr. Beigel, the jeweler was one of the friendliest greeters at church on Sunday. He would always greet the kids, too.

"Hi Joe," he called, getting Tait mixed up with his older brother.

Tait was reluctant to correct him the first time. He just smiled and answered Mr. Beigel's questions about the family. Each time he met Mr. Beigel and answered to "Joe" it became harder and harder to correct him. It seemed foolish after so many greetings now to say his name was really Tait. So Tait was always Joe to Mr. Beigel. The odd thing was that Tait's brother Joe was also called Joe by Mr. Beigel.

Tait and all the kids liked Mr. Beigel. He had a playroom on the second floor of his brick garage at the back of his lot. In the middle of the room was a pool table and along the sides of the room were an electric bowling machine, a pinball machine and a poker table with plastic chips in a carousel case sitting on top. He also had a basketball hoop attached to the outside of the garage. The kids came and went as they passed through an alley entrance to the garage, although they were supposed to knock on the back door of the house and ask permission to use the playroom. When the second floor garage windows were lit, it was a sure sign kids were at play.

Oscar Beigel had two sons and, when they were grown, he renamed the business "Oscar Beigel and Sons Jewelers". Many small businesses were located on Xenia Avenue, as was Oscar Beigel's and St. Mary Church. Beigel's store was near Tait's home. Tait could run there in under two minutes without stopping to rest if he used the alley. Mr. Beigel had a reputation of being a very honest jeweler, and he was generous, often selling items below their worth. Local patrons were loyal customers. Mr. Beigel knew diamonds, and Tait wanted to ask him about the Hope Diamond and how a thief could sell it undetected.

Tait opened the front door of the jewelry store and a bell rang to alert Mr. Biegel that someone had come into the store. It was a small room with glass topped show cases on three sides full of jewelry and watches. Mr. Beigel came into the show room from his workroom in the back. He recognized Tait at once.

"Hi Joe! How are you doing?" Mr. Beigel asked.

"Fine," Tait answered with a lopsided smile and a little out of breath.

"What can I do for you today?"

"My mom's watch is broken," Tait said handing the watch over to Mr. Beigel.

"Looks okay on the outside," he said examining the glass crystal and the wrist band. "Your mother takes good care of her watch. There is hardly a scratch on it. I'll have to take it apart to determine why it's not running. It probably just needs cleaning."

"Can I stay and watch you fix it?" Tait asked.

"You don't know what you're asking, Joe," he said. "Cleaning is a multi-step process which takes hours. I will have little watch parts all over my desk and I can't misplace even one. I don't think it's a good idea."

"Oh," Tait said bowing his head.

"I'll tell you what. I'll show you my equipment and explain the process to you. I even have a watch apart for you to examine but not touch. Come on back," he said. "I can show you a few tricks of the trade."

"Do you cut diamonds back here?" Tait asked.

"Oh no," he laughed. "Diamond cutting is a special trade all of its own. Antwerp, Belgium and Amsterdam in the Netherlands are the traditional centers of the diamond-cutting industry. New York and Israel also are important cutting centers."

"So could you cut one if you wanted, too?"

"No, not really. Only a cutting expert with special

diamond cutting machines can cut diamonds into jewels. I couldn't do it."

"Diamonds are graded under strict lighting conditions and I try and keep my work room up to standards. The white diamonds are worth the most and reflect the colors around them. I never wear yellow shirts," he said opening his suit coat showing his white shirt. "Yellow or blue, for that matter, pulls into the stone."

"Here are my watch cleaning machines," he said pointing out his equipment. "There are four work stations. The first station is a cleaning agent that washes the parts. This second station is a rinse. And the third station is also a rinse, but the machine oscillates. The fourth station is a heater."

"A heater. Why do you need a heater?"

"The heater dries the solution off the parts so the watch doesn't rust. To go through all the stations, takes two to three hours. Here is a watch I'm working on presently. It has been cleaned. Now I must assemble and oil it."

"So this is what you do all day," Tait said analyzing the work involved.

"Repair work is my mainstay. I do gold smithing, ring sizing, and designing bracelets and necklaces in addition to selling diamonds and watches."

"Do you know anything about the Hope Diamond?" Tait asked.

"Oh yes, I'm a jeweler."

"Why would someone steal it?" Tait asked. "I mean what would he do with it?"

"I don't know. Who knows all the reasons? People don't steal money to invest I don't think," he said and giggled to himself.

"How could you sell the Hope Diamond? Who would buy it?"

"Now that's a good question. The Hope Diamond is so valuable that it's practically worthless."

"What do you mean? How can it be valuable and worthless?" asked Tait.

"Well, you need to be rich to buy it. But, if you're rich, why would you take the chance? A decent man would be foolish to get involved in a thing like that."

"So what good is it to steal it?"

"I don't know. I'm not a thief," he said and laughed. "One thing I do know is that it would take a gemologist to examine it to know if it's real and not a fake."

"Are you a gemologist?" Tait asked.

"No. There are only five registered gemologists in Dayton at this time. You have to go to college and study the art and get a degree to become a gemologist. It's the science of gems. Gemologists view and rate diamonds by color, cut, clarity and clearness, and then determine the carat weight. The Hope Diamond has an older style of cut, probably European."

"I have another Hope Diamond question," Tait said.

"Ok, go ahead."

"The Pendant surrounding the Hope Diamond consists of 16 white diamonds. The thief could cut them off and sell them, couldn't he?"

"Not really. To try and pry out the diamonds would badly damage them. Diamonds have to be sawed out with a jeweler's saw."

"You mean I couldn't just take a pair of pliers and yank them apart?"

"Diamonds break. They chip easily. You would destroy the diamonds by trying to hammer them out. It takes a jeweler's saw with a special blade. I have a jeweler's saw. Let me show you."

Tait took the saw into his hands and rubbed his fingers along the blade. "It looks like a hacksaw." Tait remembered Duck Lady at the bridge, and that Katie had said she was given a little hacksaw.

"The blade is the size of fine pencil lead. It feels a little bit rough on one edge," Mr. Beigel explained. "The blades break very easily. They are placed into the saw very tightly, and if you twist them just a little while sawing, they break."

"I thought diamonds were the hardest rocks on earth?"

"They are the hardest in terms of scratching but not toughness. They chip and break. They have one direction of hardness."

"They can cut glass!"

"If you take a diamond and cut glass it will ruin the diamond's edge. The direction of hardness is the key. If you hammered a diamond you would ruin it."

"So the Hope Diamond pendant would have to stay intact. You couldn't just pry the prongs apart from the smaller diamonds?"

"Right. A person would only destroy the diamonds trying to get them apart without a jeweler's saw," Mr. Beigel confirmed.

"Where could a thief get a jeweler's saw?" Tait questioned.

"A shifty thief could go to a manufacturer and steal one."

"Where is a manufacturer?"

"There are a couple in town. There is one above Woolworth's downtown. The jeweler's saws are lying around on top of the workbenches. Nobody normally would give them a second thought. A thief could steal one if he distracted the workers."

"A gemologist would have one, right?"

"Oh yes, he would have one, any jeweler for that matter."

"I knew a man once who had a big diamond ring. He bowled a 300 game and got the ring for a prize. He is the only man I know that has a diamond ring."

"I have one," Mr. Beigel said and showed Tait the sparkling jewel. "You don't have to bowl a perfect game to get a diamond."

"No, you have to be rich," Tait said in jest. "Where do the wealthy people in town go to buy their really big diamonds?"

"Mr. Henry Wiggleshoes is the most prominent gemologist in town. He has many rich clients who buy really expensive large diamonds. They special order them from New York."

"Did you say Wiggleshoes?" Tait asked giggling.

"Yes, that's right. His name is funny but everybody remembers it. It helped make him locally famous."

"Do you know him?"

"I've met him. His shoulders are extremely small for a man of his height of about six feet four. Well dressed always. Wears a gentleman's hat that makes him look even taller. Stands very straight on long skinny legs."

"You mean like he is on stilts?"

"Yes, exactly. Now there is a man that wears a large diamond ring. His diamond is rectangular and very distinguished. I hope you enjoyed my little tour of the shop. Did you learn anything?" Mr. Beigel asked as he showed Tait to the door.

"Yes, I did. Jewelers like you repair and clean watches and sell diamond rings and things. You don't cut diamonds," Tait said summing up his experience.

Mr. Beigel patted Tait on the back and said his mother's watch should be ready to pick up next week. Tait left the store thinking about the jeweler's saw and the man named Wiggleshoes. Walking the alley toward home he grew nervous. Jerry might be behind a garage ready to jump out at him. Tait started running and the reality of the danger puffed up his fears, spurring him to run faster. When he entered the kitchen to tell his mother the watch would be ready in a week he could hardly talk, being completely out of breath.

Chapter 9

Carillon Bells

Katie, feeling Saturday would never come, had to keep waiting. Having been ready for over an hour, she was mad at Tait for taking so long to get home from collecting his paper route money. Marcus arrived early and hung out in the kitchen with Mrs. Bolinger, who fed him snacks. Tait finally arrived and they left for the park immediately. Cyrum promised to be there. The three felt sure they would collect enough evidence against Duck Lady and the others to present their case to the police.

Tait led the way, peddling fast down the rocky,

unpaved alley. A large albino squirrel jumped out in front of him so he swerved to the right, kicking up gravel. Frightened by the speeding bicycles, the squirrel hustled up a telephone poll, its feet crackling against the wood as it rounded the poll to the oppoisite side.

"Hey, did you see that squirrel?" Tait yelled out as he slowed to let Marcus come along side.

"Yea!" Marcus said, "White ones are rare. The wind is starting to pick up and it's getting a little cooler."

"The strong wind might bring in a rain storm," Tait feared.

"You know its windy when you see squirrels rolling sideways across your lawn," Marcus said trying to get a chuckle out of Tait.

Katie was quietly riding behind the boys, staying close. Tait decided to pick up the pace. They crossed Xenia Avenue, jumped the curb to use the sidewalk, and then rode hard like a line of racers. They carefully moved into traffic, turning their heads to the side and looking back, ensuring clear distance between them and the moving cars. They reached the Stuart Street Bridge with the Carillon Bells in sight and stopped to talk.

"We're way early. It's only 10:05 A.M. We got two hours to waste," Tait said.

"Let's go skip rocks on the river," cried Marcus and started down the embankment.

"It's too steep. Don't try it," Tait yelled out, but Marcus was rolling and bouncing uncontrollably down the one-hundred-foot slope toward the river's edge. Wisely he crashed sideways, skidding to a stop on the grassy shoreline within inches of plunging into the river.

"Let's leave our bicycles here at the top of the hill by the road and go down and help Marcus," Tait told Katie.

Dried tree trunks and huge tree limbs lined the shore like white dinosaur bones. Marcus picked up a log and tossed it into the river, watching it float downstream.

"What took you guys so long?" Marcus quipped.

"You won't think it's so funny when you have to drag your bicycle up that embankment," Tait cracked back.

The water was clear enough to see the bottom of

the river a few feet out from shore. The kids looked intently for fish, turtles, crawdads or anything that moved. A small flock of Canada geese honked, warning each other of approaching danger, as they waddled around in the grass.

"Do you want to see a bunch of geese fly?" Marcus said, walking fast toward the geese.

"Leave them alone," Katie insisted. "I hope one of them bites you."

"They're just birds. They like to fly. Watch this!" Marcus ran as fast as he could toward a dozen geese. They just walk away from him, scattering in all directions. None of the birds took to flight. Tait and Katie burst into laughter as they watched Marcus running this way and that, pursuing the geese who refused to fly.

"You're just too slow, Marcus," Tait yelled out. "Maybe you need your bicycle."

"These birds just don't like to fly," yelled Katie, adding to the insult.

Marcus slipped and fell on bird droppings, getting his pants full of it. Tait and Katie watched him wipe it off his pants in disgust. Marcus cleaned his hands on the grass and then went to the shoreline for water. A B-52 bomber from Wright-Patterson Air Force Base flew overhead with a deafening roar, drowning out the sound of their voices. They watched the huge craft fly over.

"I see the atomic bombs on the wings," Marcus cried out, barely being heard.

"I thought they kept the bombs inside the plane," Katie yelled into Tait's ear.

"You're right," Tait answered back. "Atomic bombs are always carried internally. Marcus is wrong."

Another B-52 flew over following the first and then another and another. Talking was impossible. Tait waved his arms toward the top of the hill where the bicycles had been left behind, and started climbing the embankment. Marcus was crawling on his knees, pulling his bicycle up to the top. The bombers faded away in the distant sky and quiet resumed along the bank of the river.

"Let's go sit by the bells. Cyrum might be there," Tait advised.

Cyrum wasn't there. They sat on the granite ledge

looking around, hoping something would happen. Tait rolled up a newspaper from his carrier bag into a funnel.

"What are you going to do with that?" asked Katie.

"I'm going to make a megaphone. One end has a small opening and the other end is wide."

"Oh, so we are going to yell to each other like cheerleaders in case of danger, right?" Katie said.

"Wrong," Tait replied. "They are listening devices"

"Listening devices? How can that be?" Katie wondered.

" When you listen you put the small opening into your ear and you can hear a lot better. It makes your ear bigger," Tait said, showing how it worked by putting the paper megaphone into his ear.

Marcus made two and put one in each ear. "If you put one in each ear you can hear in stereo," Marcus said mocking the device.

"Go over there and hide in that cluster of bushes by the light pole and listen to Katie and I talk," Tait ordered.

Marcus strolled over to the three evergreen bushes

at the base of the light pole and hid himself in the middle. He put the paper megaphone to his ear. Tait saw Marcus disappear in the bushes and began to talk in a regular tone of voice. "Marcus is a silly old goose, a silly old goose, a silly old goose. If you hear me Marcus come out of the bush and wave to me."

Marcus came out with his hands in his armpits waving his elbows like wings, acting like a silly goose. He then waved. Obviously he had heard Tait's remarks. Tait yelled for Marcus to come back up to the bell tower to discuss their plans.

"At noon I will hide in the bushes down on the parking lot side and Marcus, you can hide where you were on the river side. Katie, you can hide up here next to the bell tower. You will be able to see everything from up here."

"What time is it?" Katie asked Tait.

"It's ten minutes before eleven. We still have about an hour to wait," Tait answered.

"Let's go visit the exhibits in Carillon Park," Marcus suggested. "We've got an hour."

"I don't want to cut it too close. We've got to be back by 11:30A.M." Tait insisted.

"Ok, let's go," Marcus said and started off.

A cluster of white feathers, all that remained of a bird, lay on the ground in a circle.

"Look!" said Tait. "A hawk or an owl caught a bird here recently. Look at all the feathers. I think the hawk plucks out the feathers and then takes the body away to eat it."

"So that's why only feathers are on the ground," Katie said, comprehending the facts. Katie knelt down to gather a feather or two as a souvenir as the boys left.

The buildings of the park were nestled among the trees. As they approached, large brown sycamore leaves tumbled along the ground swirling in the wind.

"There is a log cabin." Marcus read the plaque and said, "It's Newcom Tavern, the oldest building in Dayton."

"Go over to the Wright Cycle Shop," Tait advised, pointing in the direction of another building."

"One of the Wright Brother's airplanes is here,"

Katie said. "It is the real one."

"It's not the first airplane," Tait said.

"When was it built?" Marcus asked.

Katie looked into the window of the building and read the sign. "It was built in 1905. It's the first airplane to have a passenger. It's the Wright Flyer III."

"Let's get back to the bell tower. Come on," Tait urged, getting them to focus on the detective work.

"Cyrum should be here by now," Marcus grumbled.

"Let's count the bells," Katie suggested.

Katie counted 40-bells and Marcus counted 39.

Tait was forced to count to determine who was right. Tait counted 40 bells but Marcus refused to accept it so he began counting again.

The arrival of an an orange pickup truck ended the dispute. It pulled up and stopped along the river. The truck engine continued running; exhaust was coming out of the exhaust pipe at the rear of the truck. From time to time, the drivers' face could be seen peering out through the glass of the truck window.

"I'll go read the sign on the side of the truck,"

hollered Marcus as he ran off.

"Hide in the bushes," ordered Tait. Marcus waved his hand as an okay signal without looking back.

Marcus was back again in a jiffy. The sign on the door of the truck read, "Waste Supply and Treatment."

"Okay. This might be the crooks. Marcus you go back and hide in the bushes and listen in on their conversations with your paper megaphone. If you hear anything …"

"Look, Tait!" Katie interrupted. "There is a black Cadillac that just pulled up and parked in the lot on the other side. It looks like the same one we saw at the bridge."

"I'll go hide in the bushes over by the Cadillac and listen. Katie, you stay up here next to the bell tower. Stay low so they can't see you. Keep your eyes and ears open for anything important."

From the bushes, Tait could see the truck in the distance but could not hear anything, not even with his megaphone. He hoped Marcus could pick up on the conversations being so much closer. He noticed a woman

get out of the orange truck. She waddled as she walked.
He knew it was Duck Lady. She was walking straight
toward him. Tait squatted down to be sure he was not
seen. He put the listening device to his ear.

"Do you have the white diamonds?" a male voice
asked from the Cadillac.

"Yes, here they are. All sixteen," Duck Lady
answered.

"Good! Some are pear-shaped and some are
cushion cuts," a male voice said.

"What about the necklace chain?"

"They didn't give me a chain. Only these," she
said.

Tait looked out of the bushes and through the car
window. The man in the car was examining the diamonds
with a magnifying glass.

"The men want their money. Do you have it?" she
asked.

"Yes, here is the money."

Tait looked up again and saw the man hand a bag to
Duck Lady.

"Next time I want to see the actual Hope Diamond. Give the men this note. It's sealed in the envelope. Once they read it, have them destroy it," the voice said. "It is the arrangement for our next meeting."

"Okay, Mr. Wiggleshoes," she said.

"Don't use my name," he said angrily. "Use the code name, John."

"Sorry, I forgot," she apologized.

Tait was busting with the news. He couldn't wait to tell Marcus and Katie. He was shaking with excitment and fear, knowing that if Wiggleshoes spotted him he would be in great danger.

"We need to know what is written on that note," Tait thought to himself. "We need to know when and where the next meeting is going to be held." Duck Lady started walking back to the trucks. The Cadillac drove off. Tait decided to chance it and go join Marcus in the bushes by the trucks. He walked to the bells, not in the direction of the trucks so as not to arouse suspicion.

"Did you hear anything?" Tait asked Katie.

"Nothing," she replied.

"I'm going to hide with Marcus. You stay here."

Once inside the cover of the bushes, Tait asked Marcus if he had heard anything.

"Nothing yet," he said.

"Duck Lady has a note she is giving to the men. We need ..."

"Shush," Marcus quieted Tait and put the paper listening device to his ear. Tait did the same. The front window of the truck on the passenger side opened. A head poked out and looked around. The face was familiar.

"Jerry is in the truck," Tait informed Marcus.

Duck Lady handed the driver the letter as he lowered the front window on the driver's side. The man opened the letter with his his index finger and moaned.

"Dang it!" he said, mad. "Got a paper cut."

"Hurry up and read it," Jerry demanded.

The man coughed on the first word, cleared his throat, and began to read again, "We are to meet in an empty house over on Park Avenue."

"When?" Jerry demanded and spoke very sternly.

"Next Friday night, 9:00 o'clock."

Duck Lady timidly asked, "When do I get my money?"

"After we get ours," the driver of the truck said, staring her in the face annoyed. "I'll let you know."

"Who's the driver," asked Marcus, standing up to get a better look. "I think it's the guy we saw at the bridge. A maintenance worker, I suspect."

Suddenly the truck door opened and Jerry yelled back at the driver. "I spotted a couple of snooping kids in the bushes. Help me catch them."

The truck doors slammed shut as the men came at Tait and Marcus. Duck Lady stood still, quacking softly, lifting her feet up and down nervously.

Both boys headed to their bicycles. Katie panicked and ran to Tait and Marcus instead of to the bikes.

"Get the girl, get the girl," the one man said. "She will be easy to catch."

Tait became furious when the men began chasing Katie. He picked up a stick, turned and ran right at the two men challenging them to chase him or be hit in the head by the stick. Katie, energized by fear, ran with lightning speed, jerking herself left and then right like a rabbit to avoid the grabbing hands of her pursuer.

"You little squirt," the man said chasing her. "You're faster than I thought."

Suddenly the men stopped chasing the kids. "Hey," one yelled. "There is some crazy black guy throwing rocks at my company truck."

The two men forgot about the kids as they ran to the truck. They stopped together on the bank of the river, and watched the fleeing black man.

"I know that guy," Jerry told his partner. "I swear I'm going to kill that son of a gun."

"Who is it?"

"They call him, 'Tin Can Man'." Jerry looked around for the kids and spotted them riding swiftly out of the park. It started to drizzle.

"Let's get out of here," Jerry instructed his partner and they got into the truck and drove off forsaking the kids.

Marcus yelled out, "We better hurry. If it rains

hard, we will get all wet, and it's cold."

Suddenly Tait hit his brakes, doing a little dance with his bicycle, and then fell to the concrete sidewalk. Marcus and Katie turned around and went back.

" What are you doing now?" Katie asked.

I got my gym-shoe lace caught in the sprocket of my bike. It got wrapped around the pedal bar."

"You've been hanging around Marcus too long," Katie said jokingly.

"Very funny," Marcus said in a stern voice. "I'm a much better rider than that."

A jogger jumped over Tait and his fallen bicycle yelling, "Excuse me" which caused Tait to pinch his finger on the sprocket.

"Jiminy Crickets," Tait said angrily. "Some people have no courtesy.

"Nervous, Tait," Marcus said laughing.

"Yes, I'm nervous. We know a lot now about this case and they know where I live. We need to talk with Cyrum."

"It's starting to rain harder. We better get going,"

Katie urged.

"I've almost got the lace untangled. Give me a second," Tait said irritated.

They arrived home all wet, cold and hungry. A change of clothing and a hot meal had Tait bubbling for action. He wanted to talk with Cyrum in the worst way.

Chapter 10

Duck Lady

"I think we should tell mom what's going on," Katie suggested to Tait.

"We will. Let me talk to Cyrum first," Tait insisted.

"Okay, but call now," Katie answered sternly.

Tait called Cyrum on the phone and Cyrum explained that he had seen the whole thing at Carillon park from his car. Dennis Tucker's rock throwing was clever he thought.

"Should we go to the police now?" Tait asked.

"We need to tie up some loose ends," Cyrum counseled.

"Let's meet and talk this out," proposed Tait.

"Okay, let's talk. Tomorrow is Sunday. After you deliver your paper route meet me at the river again. You,

Marcus, and Katie stay in a group and be in the open where other people can see you," Cyrum advised.

"Should I bring my fishing stuff?"

"Yes, that way people will think that's all we are doing."

Tait got his newspapers for delivery at the branch garage early the next morning and rode toward his first customer's house. Not many cars were on the streets. When he heard the noise of car tires behind him, he took notice. Expecting the car to pass, he stayed close to the curb. It didn't pass, but slowed down to his speed. Tait left the street to ride on the sidewalk. The car came to the curb. Immediately Tait worried it was Jerry trying to run him over. He turned and went down an alley. The car followed. He took a short cut through a yard and out on the next block. Tait saw the car turning the corner to get to him. Tait peddled like never before. The car came up along side with its window down and the man yelled out.

"Hey, I'd like to buy a paper! Would you please stop?"

Tait suddenly realized that it wasn't Jerry after all.

Tait discreetly handed a paper through the passenger side window, all the while looking the man in the face to discern possible trouble. The man gave him a dollar and said keep the tip. The man drove off with no further interest in Tait. Solving crimes was beginning to lose its appeal. Tait was beginning to feel like he was the one being hunted.

It only took a half hour for Tait to finish his route. The kids arrived at the river and were greeted by a big friendly smile which calmed them all down a little.

"Well, well, well, look who came fishing," Cyrum said with boisterous affection."

They were all there just like the Sunday before, listening to the waterfall and looking up at the railroad bridge.

"I heard Duck Lady call the man in the Cadillac Mr. Wiggleshoes," Tait informed Cyrum, taking a deep breath while getting off his bike. "He got mad at her for using his real name."

"Good work. You really are a detective. Did you hear anything else?" Cyrum questioned.

"Wiggleshoes is going to buy the Hope Diamond

next Friday," Katie said excitedly.

"Where is the meeting?"

"In an empty house over on Park Avenue," said Marcus.

"What time?" Cyrum asked.

"Nine o'clock."

"In the morning?"

"No, at night."

"Good work by all of you. I need to figure out where this empty house is located. Also, I would like to know the name of the maintenance man who works at the waste treatment plant," Cyrum explained.

"What should we do?" Tait asked.

"Relax! Get you some red worms out of my little bucket there and fish. God's paradise," he said as he waved his arms in delight. So let's enjoy it."

"Boy, you're sure in a good mood," Tait said, jarred at the change in Cyrum's temperament.

"We will have these guys behind bars as soon as I gather a few more facts."

Katie bent down and picked up a worm and put it

on her hook. She threw out her line and gave Cyrum a look.

"Good for you, little woman," he said. "Don't let a little worm scare you."

"I think it's a little too dangerous for you kids right now to continue to gather information. Let me do it. We can go to the police and let them do the dirty work," Cyrum said thoughtfully.

"How you going to find out anything?" Tait asked.

"I'm going to talk with Dennis Tucker. He can mix with the street people. I can do some undercover work also. I'll get back in touch with you kids later."

"Where you going to go?" Marcus asked.

"Dennis can go to the river and check out who is sleeping under the bridges. Somebody might know the name of the maintenance worker."

"That's not very important," Tait said. "We will catch him when we catch the others."

"True, but it might help our case with the police. The important thing is to locate the empty meeting house. I'll walk that neighborhood haunt at night."

"Look! Look over there," Katie said pointing. "There is a small motor boat out in the middle of the river above the falls. Do you see it?"

"There is a frogman in the middle of the water falls," Tait reported.

"The frogman is holding onto a rope connected to the boat. Looks like he is walking the falls," Katie informed.

"The boat has Box 21 written on the side. That's a rescue unit," Cyrum said. "The man is a scuba diver. See the air tanks on his back?"

"Uh, oh! The boat's motor quit. The two men in the boat are frantically pulling on the motor cord trying to get it started again," Tait said anxiously.

"That scuba diver is in trouble," Marcus said putting down his fishing pole. "He's pulling on the rope as fast as he can, trying to keep himself from falling down into the falls."

"If they don't get that motor running, the scuba diver will pull the boat over the falls," Tait said worried.

One of the men in the boat started waving his arms,

signaling the scuba diver to let go of the rope. When the scuba diver let go of the rope, he disappeared, falling into the rushing water of the falls. The motor roared as it started, but it was too late to save the diver. The boat sped around in a circle, heading closer to the falls as the men looked for their scuba buddy.

"Do you think the scuba diver is caught below the falls in the turbulent water?" Tait asked Cyrum.

"Don't know. I hope the man got away from the falls and is swimming under the water somewhere," Cyrum said searching with his eyes.

Then, without warning, the scuba diver stood up. He looked like a giant monster coming out of the water.

"Reel in your fishing lines," yelled Cyrum. "The frogman could get his feet entangled in our lines."

He raised his feet above the water line, letting his fins flap freely. The hood on the green rubber suit covered his head. He took off his mask and walked to the shore. He fell to the ground and took off his fins and air tanks. He pulled back the rubber hood, from his head. He laid flat down on the ground, breathing hard. Cyrum ran over to him, bent down on one knee and asked him if he needed anything. He said no, that he would be all right in a minute.

"I've seen people fish the water falls before but nothing like this," Tait said.

"The scuba diver began laughing. I'm not trying to catch fish," he said.

"A lady jumped off the Stuart Street Bridge last night. Committed suicide. We think her body might be caught in the falls."

The kids looked at each other in utter amazement. Why would anyone do that?

Cyrum asked, "Do you know who she was?"

"She was a street person. She walked around downtown all the time quacking like a duck," the man said. "I'm with Box 21 Rescue Unit."

"Duck Lady committed suicide last night!" Katie said astonished.

"Did you look under the bridge?" Cyrum asked. "Drowning victims usually sink straight down."

"Yes, we did, but we didn't find the cadaver. We

think it got carried down stream."

A four-wheel drive pickup truck arrived. The driver got out and started talking with the scuba diver. He helped the diver gather his gear and put it in the bed of the truck. They left.

"Cyrum," Tait said as they all stood there in shock. "I don't think that was a suicide. I think it was murder."

"I think you're right," Cyrum agreed.

"Now I know this is too dangerous for you kids. Let me handle this. I'll meet you three at Wympee's restaurant on Thursday after school, about 3:30 P.M. That will give me a little time to gather the information I need. Hopefully it will be enough to convince the police. Do you know where the Wympee restaurant is located?"

"Yes, I've been there," Tait said.

"Don't get caught alone for the next few days. Jerry is a killer," Cyrum cautioned. "Stay together."

Tait realized that the capture of these men was beyond anything he could do alone. The police were required. Even Cyrum needed to be careful.

Chapter 11

Wympee's Restaurant

Sitting quietly at his desk at school on Thursday, Tait found himself daydreaming about Duck Lady, Jerry, and the meeting with Cyrum at Wympee's restaurant.

"Tait!" the teacher called out after pointing to a map. "What is the capital of this state?"

"Columbus," he replied.

"Columbus is the capital of Ohio, the state in which you live, but it is not the capital of New York," she said and the whole class laughed boisterously. Tait suffered through the belittlement. He was more interested in meeting Marcus between classes.

"Marcus!" Tait yelled when he saw him in the hall. "Are you coming to Wympee's or not?"

"No," Marcus answered.

"Why not?"

"I think I saw Jerry outside the school. I'm not taking any chances."

"If we stick together we will be okay," Tait said harshly. "Cyrum is expecting us."

Marcus just stood there uncooperative and negative.

"You're not chicken are you?"

"Those are fighting words," Marcus said clenching his fist.

"Okay, okay," Tait said backing off. "I'll buy you a Fat Boy with fries if you come."

Marcus thought about it and said, "If I get a large chocolate malt too, it's a deal."

"Deal," Tait agreed, just as the bell rang for them to get to their next class.

After school, Tait and Marcus raced across the playground to get their bikes. They began racing toward home and were stride for stride dead-even when Marcus tripped and fell face down between first and second base on the all dirt ball diamond. Tait stopped and came back. Marcus stood up, dusted off his trousers, and then raced to the sidewalk to declare victory.

"That's not fair and you know it," Tait cried while watching Marcus jump up and down in victory.

Somehow Katie had beat both of them home and was sitting on her bike waiting. Still in their school clothes, they cycled through the narrow side streets of the downtown to Wympee's. Tait's leg muscles began to burn from the strain of pushing too hard for too long up hill. At the top of the hill he coasted so they could catch up.

"Do you think Cyrum is ready to go to the police yet?" Katie inquired.

"Yep," Tait replied. "Sometimes police officers eat at Wympee's. Cyrum probably has plans for us to meet with the police there."

When they turned onto Wayne Avenue from

Richard Street, Tait yelled out, "The street is flat all the way to Third Street. It's easy going from here."

"Is the restaurant on Third Street?" Katie asked.

"Yeah, another five blocks. Ten city blocks is a mile, dad says, so we got another half mile to go."

They parked their bikes behind the building and walked to the front door, past three metal newspaper stands. The door swung in. Tait ducked to avoid hitting his head on a metal coat rack tree that was out of place. Tait repositioned the tree out of the way and got a glance from a waitress as she hustled through the kitchen door backwards carrying dirty dishes. The three kids stood waiting to be escorted to their seats.

"There are twenty-seven stools," Tait told Marcus after carefully counting both sides of the restaurant. "Eleven stools face the kitchen and sixteen face the street."

"So?" said Marcus.

"Observe," Tait said with an air of intelligence and gave everything the once-over like a detective.

"I just want to sit down and eat," Marcus replied.

Another waitress, slim and energetic, marched down between the stools talking as she walked. "More coffee, Jake? How about you, Don?" she said, pouring hot coffee into their cups before they even answered. Spilling coffee, she simply wiped it up with the towel she carried around her waist. "Chilly today, isn't it?" The men had kept their coats on and were staring out the window at the moving traffic.

Sirens filled the air as a fire engine with ladders stretching out the back of the truck and a police cruiser went by. Marcus opened the door for a better look.

"Did you see that?" Marcus hollered.

"Yes," Katie answered. "You act like you never saw a fire engine before.

A slender bow-legged cowboy with well wore jeans and boots went over to the far corner and put a dime into the juke box. Country-western music was the favorite music of the people who visited Wympee's.

A number of folded newspapers, already read by previous customers, were flung on the counter and stools for people to read.

"Just sit anywhere," the waitress hollered out.

"Look in the corner, Marcus," said Tait as he started walking to a seat.

A man was sitting on the last stool in the corner by the cigarette machine opposite the cash register. His head was hidden behind the sports section of a newspaper. The man looked out the window, and then continued reading. Tait recognized the unshaven face of the train-hopping bum.

Tait guided Katie and Marcus to the other end of the restaurant opposite the juke box. The three sat on the very last stools facing the windows dwarfed beside two huge construction workers. The stools, bolted to the floor very close together, forced them to share elbow room. The round tops of the stools spun around and the three kids were testing the action. Tait leaned on the counter top and put his head close to Katie. Marcus leaned in, too.

"Do you recognize that guy at the other end of the room by the cigarette machine reading a newspaper?" Tait asked, compelling a look.

Katie couldn't see around the two construction workers so she got off her seat and peered around the men.

"It's Jerry," Katie cried, frightened.

The kids watched him sip his coffee, take a whiff on his cigarette and continue reading his paper.

"Cyrum is supposed to be here. Where is he?" Marcus grumbled, alarmed.

"He will be here. Don't worry," Tait said. A nice looking waitress with a pony-tail came over and sat down on the stool by Marcus. "What can I get you kids today?" she asked cheerfully.

"Do you have a menu?" Katie asked.

"Sure, just a minute." She walked away and came back with three small plastic menu cards. "Here you go. Do you want a minute?"

"Yes," answered Tait.

A large portion of the menu listed different types of hamburgers. The Fatty Burger was first on the list and Marcus said he was ready to order almost instantly.

"They have a fish sandwich," Katie said, reading

further down the menu.

"Who would want a fish sandwich when you can have a Fatty Burger," Marcus questioned. "It would take three fish sandwiches to satisfy me."

"They would have to be whale sandwiches to satisfy you," added Tait.

"You can still order breakfast," Katie said, entertaining thoughts of something different. "Biscuits and gravy, yum!"

"The special today is liver and onions with whipped potatoes. That ought to fill you up, Marcus," Tait said in jest.

"I hate liver. That's dog food. I want a Fatty Burger with fries like you promised," he said with decisiveness.

A half-dozen flower pots rested on the window ledge between the sugar jars, napkin holders, catsup bottles, and salt and pepper shakers.

Tait reached for a napkin and Marcus started playing with the salt and pepper shakers when the waitress yelled over, "I'll be with you in a minute."

A man wearing painters bib overalls with multi-colors of paint splashed over the white suit came in and sat down facing the kitchen. He wore no coat, but left his painters cap on, which was splattered predominatly with white house paint. He ordered a coke and then began to drink through the straw. He stroked his chin as if in self-thought. He never glanced around at all. Tait knew he was a regular when the cook yelled out in a deep grizzly voice to the man, "Do you want fries buddy?" as if it was the man's standard order.

"Yeah," was the reply.

The waitress, suddenly upon them, asked, "Okay, what do you want to order."

"I'll take a Fatty Boy with fries," Marcus said.

"You mean the dinner," she asked.

"What comes with the dinner?" Marcus asked confused.

"A Fatty boy, fries, and cold slaw," she replied. "It's cheaper that way."

"Okay," he said.

"I'll have a cheese burger with fries and a chocolate

malt," Tait requested.

"Oh yeah! I'll take a malt too," Marcus interrupted.

"I'll take a cheese and ham omelet, orange juice, and two pieces of toast," Katie said, ordering with a sense of certainty.

"Gee, what are you trying to do? Make me go broke?" Tait asked a little irrately, knowing he was paying for her meal, too.

"It doesn't cost anymore than the Fatty Boy dinner," she said defending herself.

"Where is that Cyrum?" Marcus complained again. "He said he was going to disappear but not forever."

"He didn't say disappear. He said undercover. He'll be here. Just be patient," Tait said realizing he was talking like his mother.

Conversations picked up and Tait could hear bits and pieces of sentences spoken loud and with intensity.

"I worked twenty-two years there … the best part of my life… they let me go," one man said explaining his situation to a friend.

Out the window Tait saw a large barrel chested

woman waddling her huge bottom from side-to-side moving toward the entrance of the restaurant followed by a short skinny man wearing a Cincinnati Reds ball cap. They came into the place. Their entering was like that of celebrities.

"Roberta! Long time no see," came a cry from a older gentleman sitting alone.

"How you doing.?." the man with the ball cap said to the customer as he came through the door.

"Good. How you doing?" was the reply.

"Nice day today," the woman added.

"You got that right," the man said and laughed through his nose.

A waitress escorted the big women to a large chair off to the side like it was her special place.

The kid's food arrived. Marcus devoured the huge Fatty Boy like it was a cookie and gulped down his chocolate malt like it was a beer. Katie delicately spread butter on her toast letting it melt and ate like a lady. Tait munched his cheeseburger and listened in on all the conversations.

"I was talking to a guy the other day ... ," got Tait's ear and then "I really don't mind ...," came in his other ear. The disconnected thoughts made no sense at all to Tait, but he could not turn his ears off.

" ...just came from the doctor. I had scratched it ...swollen...I'm getting blood work done..."

Tait analyzed the broken conversations that filled the small room. Each person that spoke revealed a little about himself. Soon Tait felt comfortable with the crowd except for Jerry.

Katie elbowed Tait and pointed outside to a man putting change into the newspaper rack. "Isn't that Wiggleshoes? He is wearing a huge rectangular diamond ring."

Tait almost choked on his sandwich when he realized it was true. "It's Wiggleshoes."

"What's he doing here?" Marcus snarled, posturing himself defensively.

Wiggleshoes put the newspaper under his arm and looked through the window of the restaurant. Jerry put his newspaper on the counter top and waved ever so slightly

152

to Wiggleshoes as a sign he saw him. Wiggleshoes walked out of sight toward the back of the building. Jerry got up and went to the cash register.

"They're going to have a meeting outside, I bet you," Marcus said and jumped up bumping the huge man sitting next to him. The man glanced back but then continued talking to his buddy.

Tait tried to sit Marcus down again, but it was too late. Jerry spotted them, and gave Tait a long stare, obviously considering doing something. The waitress took Jerry's money and gave him change without a word.

"Wait Marcus," Tait cried out. "I have to pay."

"Where is Cyrum when you need him?" Marcus grumbled again with panic in his voice.

Jerry hesitated before going out the door, slowly putting his bills into his wallet. He glanced around, possibly looking for Cyrum but then glanced again in Tait's direction. He jerked the door open with power and left.

"Marcus you leave the tip. I'll pay for everything else," Tait advised.

Marcus left a small tip of coins and then began eating the remains of Tait's cheeseburger.

"Marcus, come on!" Tait demanded as he opened the door.

"We can't waste all this food. We paid good money for this," Marcus grunted.

Tait and Katie went outside while Marcus stuffed his pockets with French fries. He darted down the row of stools to the door dropping fries every few feet.

"Where is that Cyrum?" Marcus complained again as he approached Tait. "He should be here by now."

"Maybe they got him," Katie said fearing the worst.

They went and stood with their bicycles. Tait noticed the Cadillac parked up against the building across the lot. Jerry got out of the car and started their way.

"Run for it," Marcus yelled out as he grabbed his bicycle. He leaped onto the seat while the bike was in motion, like a cowboy jumping on a horse in full gallop.

The big lady came out of the restaurant waving her hands for them to stop but Tait rushed Katie into motion.

They peddled as fast as they could go. Tait looked

back and noticed the Cadillac pull out of the parking lot heading their way. He didn't notice the big lady pointing to her partner in the Red's ball cap to go across the street to a car.

"They're following us," yelled Tait. "Stay close together. Do everything I do and go wherever I go."

Chapter 12

Cemetery

The three young cyclists zoomed down Wayne Avenue close together as a unit. Tait was desperately trying to think of a plan of escape. The Cadillac passed them and stopped along the curb just beyond the corner. Jerry got out of the car and quickly ran on foot toward the kids, intending to knock them off their bikes. Tait, in unison with the others, made a sharp right turn. Jerry missed and returned to the car. They rode furiously down Jackson Street. Tait circled back, down alleys to Wayne Avenue, in an attempt to confuse and lose their would-be attackers. The three raced through the light at Fifth Street as it turned yellow, and Tait, looking back, spotted the Cadillac stopped on red.

An old Ford pulled out from a side street behind the bikers. Tait left the curb lane and rode in the middle of the street.

"Ride side by side," Tait ordered.

Cars began to honk their horns as they held up traffic. The Cadillac was stuck two cars back, unable to pass.

"We can't hold up traffic forever," Marcus shouted. "Now what are we going to do?"

Tait made another sharp right turn, this time down Hickory Street, a narrow side street. Tait was familiar with the neighborhood, since he knew Emerson School was located on Hickory. The Cadillac approached quickly. Tait made a hard left down Perrine Street across from the school, with Katie and Marcus in his wind. The Cadillac slid past the intersection, breaking heavily and leaving tracks of rubber. The engine roared as the car backed up and continued the pursuit. Tait went though an open fence-gate through a private yard to an alley with

Katie and Marcus so close they were almost touching wheels.

At Cross Street, which dead ends into Wyoming, Tait stopped to discuss a plan. The Cadillac was not in sight.

"We'll lose them in the cemetery," Tait explained. "I know how to get in. The fence at the corner of the cemetery is broken and pushed down at the top. We can climb over easy. Let's go."

"How far away is it?" Katie asked.

"Just up ahead. Wyoming Street runs along the edge of Woodland Cemetery."

Tait climbed over the fence first. Marcus handed the bikes over the top to Tait, and then Katie and Marcus climbed over. The three of them marched up the forested, steep hillside dragging their bicycles.

A thunderous voice hollered, "I see them!"

"It's Jerry!" cried Katie from the top of the hill.

Jerry had climbed the fence and was starting up the hill, when he was called back by Wiggleshoes.

At the top of the hill a narrow road meandered

throughout the park to the various burial sections.

"Goose Lake is at the bottom of the hill down this road. We can hide out there and rest," Tait told the others.

"How do you know that?" Marcus asked.

"My grandfather is buried here and my dad drove us all around this cemetery. There are a lot of famous people buried here."

At the far end of Goose Lake, they got off their bikes and laid them flat behind a monument. They sat with their backs against a huge tombstone, the lake behind them, and considered what to do next.

"I think we lost them," Tait said hopefully.

"Mom is going to be mad. Look at my slacks. Grass stains on the knees, and these were my best school clothes," Katie said sadly.

"She'll be happy you're not dead," Tait said trying to cheer her up.

"Anybody want some fries?" Marcus quipped as he removed cold fries from his pockets.

"Yuck, no, thanks," said Katie sticking out her

tongue and pretending to vomit.

"Where is Cyrum?" Marcus asked harshly. "He's the one that told us to meet at Wympee's. He disappears and leaves up hanging."

"I think they got him." Katie suggested. They killed Duck Lady, didn't they?" she said to prove her point. "Now they're after us."

"Maybe we should make a mad dash for home," proposed Marcus.

"The Cadillac might be sitting at the fence corner waiting for us. We're going to have to wait here for awhile," Tait advised.

"Until dark," Katie said sulkily. Mom and Dad will be furious."

"I'm shivering. Let's go someplace out of the wind," Marcus suggested.

"Okay," Tait agreed. "We can push our bikes up to Lookout Point. It's the highest point in Dayton. We will be able to see everything from up there. Maybe we can find a warmer place."

As they lumbered uphill, Katie read the names

engraved on old gray stone markers, hoping to run across a famous person.

"Here is a grave from 1846," Katie announced. The Wright Brothers graves are around here someplace."

"Just keep walking," Marcus ordered. "We don't have time for sightseeing."

"All these hills are glacial moraine," Katie explained. "I just learned that in science class."

"Thanks," Marcus commented. "I've always wanted to know that."

The Cadillac suddenly appeared, coming toward them slowly, progressing up the narrow twisting park road.

"Everybody split up. Let's meet at Lookout Point," Tait yelled, and trotted higher up the incline. The ground leveled off so he rode through the grass between the gravestones putting distance between him and the Cadillac.

After an arduous climb up another hill, Tait found a large grave monument in the shape of a cross with an angel in front large enough to hide him and his bike. He hid behind the angel peering out at the road, wondering if Katie and Marcus escaped. The Cadillac rolled on by, almost silently, as Tait examined the occupants in the car. Katie's tearful face could be seen staring out the back seat window. She had been captured.

Tait waited until the car was out of sight and then pushed his bike upward to Lookout Point. Hopefully Marcus would be there. Steps of stone led the way to the top of the lookout, with large boulders all along the sides of the hill.

Tait put his bike flat on the ground and laid belly down to keep from being seen. Only his head popped up from time to time to look for Marcus and to view the road for the Cadillac. Tait thought to ride down hill to the main gate and escape, but he couldn't leave without Marcus.

Twenty feet below on the road that curved around the knoll of Lookout Point, the Cadillac came creeping like a tiger ready to pounce on its prey.

Tait looked through the back window of the car to check if Katie was all right. To his surprise, Marcus was seated next to her.

Infuriated and determined to get revenge, Tait lifted a large boulder and tossed it down at the windshield of the automobile, hoping it would crash through the window and injure the driver and Jerry. The boulder bounced off the glass and rested on the hood of the car. The windshield was damaged leaving a spider web crack over the entire portion of the driver's viewing area. The boom sounded like a bomb exploding, Jerry leaped out of the car and stared up at Tait.

Jerry started his ascent and Tait grabbed his bicycle and headed the other way down the steps. Jumping on his bike, he glided downhill leaning into the sharp curves of the zigzagging Woodland Park road. With gravity on his side, he figured he could beat them to the main entrance to the cemetery and lose them in the alleys and backyards of the neighborhood.

The road was steep and had a turnabout snaking right. Tait had to slow down and reverse his direction. Jerry came over the crest of the turnabout on foot, running hard and jumping onto the road in front of Tait. Tait swerved, hit a stone grave marker and flipped. The bum was on top of him in a flash. He too was caught.

Pushed into the back seat of the car, he caught the despairing eyes of Marcus. Tait grew more determined. The two men drove the vehicle around the cemetery and discussed what to do with the kids. Marcus thought they were just trying to scare them, but Tait knew better.

"Mr. Wiggleshoes," Tait mumbled through his gag. "Let's make a deal."

"The kid knows my name. How do you know my name, kid?" he demanded.

"I guessed," Tait answered coyly.

Jerry turned his body and looked at the kids in the back seat. "Do you know my name?"

"Jerry, " he muttered, and immediately regretted revealing too much.

"What else do you know about me?" Wiggleshoes asked attempting to flush information out of Tait.

"Nothing," Tait replied knowing it wise to say little.

"We know you are going to buy the Hope Diamond, that's what," Marcus hollered through his gag.

Tait grimaced. Marcus' big mouth said just what

164

Mr. Wiggleshoes wanted to find out. He pinched Marcus, communicating his displeasure.

"These kids know too much. They will have to be eliminated."

"What are we going to do with them?" Jerry asked.

"See that crypt over yonder?"

"Yes, I get it. We lock them up in an old mausoleum. Make it look like an accident. They'll be dead in a few days," Jerry said agreeing on the plan.

The car stopped and the two men got out and examined the pad lock on the iron doors of an Egyptian style crypt.

"Can you break it?" the well dressed Wiggleshoes asked.

"Oh sure, I can break it. All I need is a large rock," Jerry said and started looking around.

Mr. Wiggleshoes started pacing and looking around nervously and said, "I don't like this. Let's go."

"What are we going to do with the kids," questioned Jerry.

"Duck Lady had an accident didn't she?"

"Yes, that was easy. All I had to do was push her off the bridge," Jerry said showing no remorse.

"This will be easy, too. The kids are going to have a little swimming accident. They will drown in the falls tonight."

"I'm telling you now. I need a bigger share of the money for doing the dirty work. Double my share," Jerry said, giving an ultimatum.

"Okay, okay! Just do as I say."

"When do I get it? I mean all the money?" Jerry said, provoked by the extra pressure on him to dispose of the kids.

"Tomorrow night when we make the Hope Diamond exchange in the old abandoned house."

"Good. I plan to vanish down south where it's warm and enjoy my good fortune."

"It will be dark in a couple of hours. We will just drive around and then go to the railroad bridge by the falls. It shouldn't take long," Wiggleshoes explained. He stepped on the gas and sped through a yellow traffic light turned red.

"Don't do that," warned Jerry. "All we need is to get stopped by the police with a car full of kids.

The car stopped at the next red light. People were crossing the intersection so Tait started wiggling and moving wildly in the back seat.

"Hey! Help us!" Tait yelled through his gag.

Marcus managed to remove his gag. He stuck his nose against the glass and hollered, "Help! We are prisoners." A pedestrian glanced over but kept walking.

Jerry reacted by punching Marcus between the eyes, knocking him unconscious. He back-handed Tait across the face, causing blood to run from his nose. Katie sat motionless. Knowing the end was near, their only hope was Cyrum.

As time passed, Tait kept looking out the window trying to keep track of where they were but finally gave up. Marcus changed position, shook his head and opened his eyes, "Where are we?" Nobody answered. The Cadillac parked above the river near the train bridge with the motor running and the headlights off.

"Here is a flashlight," Mr. Wiggleshoes said.

"Don't forget to get the bicycles out of the trunk and park them by the falls. It's a twenty-five foot drop to the falls. Throw each kid out as far as possible. They should get caught in the turbulence of the water at the base of the falls. Box 21 Rescue Unit will retrieve them tomorrow and everyone will think it was an accident."

Jerry opened his door and put one leg out when a ferocious dog charged from the darkness, growling to kill.

"Holy Smokes!" yelled Jerry. There's a wild German Shepherd out there ready to tear my leg off!"

"Here," Mr. Wiggleshoes said as he handed him a gun. "Kill it."

Jerry opened the window a crack to aim a bullet at the dog, but the dog kept jumping up flashing his white teeth at the man's hand.

"I can't even open the window. That's a mad dog out there."

"Give me the gun," Mr. Wiggleshoes demanded. "I'll kill it."

Mr. Wiggleshoes opened the door quickly and got out. The dog ran around the car to his side. Bang!

Wiggleshoes hit the ground with a thud and a great commotion ensued.

"What's going on out there?" Jerry yelled.

No answer.

The dog was quiet. Jerry scooted over to the driver's side and looked into the darkness shining the light beam of his flashlight all around.

"Jerry!" yelled Mr. Wiggleshoes from the ground. "It's the black man! Kill him!"

"It's Cyrum out there," Katie cried frantically.

Jerry got out of the car and the dog attacked with a fury. Tait strained to see.

"It is Cyrum! He's fighting with Wiggleshoes over the gun."

Jerry jumped on Cyrum and Wiggleshoes fired a shot. The dog yelped once and lay still.

"Shoot him!" growled Jerry. "Shoot him!"

Another shot was heard and the battle was over. Cyrum rolled down hill to the river.

"Let's get out of here," yelled Mr. Wiggleshoes.

"What about the kids?"

"It's too late. The plan won't work now. A dead dog. A dead black man and three drowned white kids. The police would track us down. We have to change our plan. Get in the car," he demanded.

"The police are going to investigate the death of the black man," Jerry said coughing and spitting and then getting into the car.

"They won't give it much attention. A black rail-riding hobo got shot. That's all. The dog however, they might get upset about," he said chuckling.

They turned the headlights back on and drove away fast.

"You have blood on your coat," Jerry said. "You need to get cleaned up."

"Tait, they shot Cyrum. Oh how I wish I were home," said Katie.

Tait squeezed her hand and said softly, "Don't give up. It's dark out there. Maybe Cyrum got away."

Chapter 13

The Exchange

The Cadillac moved slowly down the river road blowing up dust before turning right and proceeding through a short tunnel. "Where are we going?" Jerry asked upset about the turn of events.

"We can lock the kids up in the abandoned house on Park Avenue. You can stay and guard them until I come up with another plan. I need to get cleaned up. There is no running water there, so I'll have to go home."

"I never bargained for all this. I …"

"Shut up. You're in this same as me. We will dispose of the kids and exchange the diamond tomorrow night."

The electricity was turned off. Mr. Wiggleshoes used his flashlight to pass through a back pantry void of all furniture to enter the kitchen. A camper's lantern sat on the table. Four wooden chairs were scattered about the room. Mr. Wiggleshoes took out a match, bent over, and lit the lantern, which blazed brightly. He turned the light down and stood erect.

"Sit here," he demanded of the children, pointing to the kitchen chairs.

"Tie them up good and tight," he ordered Jerry. "I don't want any funny business going on. If they try to escape, knock them out with your fist."

"Hey, when are you coming back? I can't stay here all night and all day without food and water," Jerry retorted.

"I'll be back in a few hours and bring something to eat and a beer. That ought to make you happy."

"What about these kids? What are we going to do with them?"

"I told you I'd come up with a plan," Mr. Wiggleshoes said fuming. "Your job is to sit here and guard these kids. I need to get my windshield fixed in the morning and get ready for the exchange. Don't panic. I'll be back."

"You better come back, and with lots of money," Jerry said as his lip twitched in anger. "My responsibilities seem to grow as the days go on."

The back door slammed, leaving the place quiet.

"I hate this waiting business," groaned Jerry as he faced the children. "Stop staring at me. Close your eyes."

Tait glanced quickly at Marcus. Both of his eyes were black now from the blow to the head earlier. Katie decided to try and doze off. Exhausted from the stress of the day she succeeded. Marcus too slouched in his chair and rested quietly. Tait remained calm and calculating with eyelids a little bit open. Shadows danced on the floor up to the wall from the burning glow of the lamp. Jerry turned down the fire in the lamp, leaving only enough light for protection against a possible escape. Jerry got restless. He got up from the table and paced the room, causing the hardwood floorboards to creak under his shoes.

Tait wiggled in his chair trying to unloose the ropes around his hands and the bum noticed. Jerry came over and placed the gun on the table in front of Tait.

"Don't even think about it, kid. If you manage to get loose, you're dead." He picked up the gun and put the barrel to Tait's nose. "Get it. You're dead."

Jerry then sat down on the floor in the doorway of the kitchen, the only escape route. Tait began to wonder about Cyrum. Was he dead? Tait was thinking of ways to escape when sleep overcame him.

When Tait awoke, the morning light was coming in through the kitchen windows and Jerry was up. The bum was peering out through the plywood covering the front door in the next room. He came in and extinguished the lantern. Everyone jumped when the back door opened.

"It's only me," boomed the voice of Mr. Wiggleshoes.

"God, you scared me," Jerry said in a rough voice. "I almost put a bullet through your head."

Mr. Wiggleshoes stood still, stunned at the thought

and then said, "I brought you donuts and coffee. I don't want you falling asleep on me."

"You should have come earlier. It's daylight now. I fought staying awake all night."

The kids got nothing to eat. They just sat and watched Jerry eat a half dozen donuts, belch repeatedly, and then give a look of satisfaction. Mr. Wiggleshoes was busy bringing in a bunch of stuff.

"What are you doing?" Jerry asked Wiggleshoes.

"I'm setting things up for tonight," he said.

"Why do you need a gasoline can?"

"The kids are going to have an accident playing with the camper's lantern. The bed upstairs will catch on fire and the whole house will burn down. These foolish kids will have a wonderful funeral, attended by many school children."

"You are a sinister, heartless fellow aren't you? You're such a good salesman with your charms and loving manner. Who would guess you're a killer?"

"Just shut up. I didn't plan it this way. It's the kids' own fault for meddling."

Mr. Wiggleshoes headed toward the back door, then stopped and turned around.

"Here! I brought you these," he said and threw a deck of cards on the table. "Just in case you get bored."

Wiggleshoes left the house with a bang of the door and all was silent. Jerry sipped on his coffee and glarred at Tait with a detesting look.

"You've had it made, kid," Jerry said with invidiousness. "When I was your age my father had left my mother, she was an alcoholic bar maid, and I stole to get enough money to eat."

Tait kept silent.

Jerry combed his smelly hair with his hand and took another sip of coffee. "I stole a bicycle when I was nine. It was the only bike I ever had. I pick-pocketed drunks at the tavern where mom worked. I raised myself." Jerry pulled out a cigarette, leaned back on his chair and smoked. He seemed to calm down.

"Do you want to play cards?" Tait asked mutely through his gag.

"Sure, kid," Jerry said. "Poker! That's all I play."

Tait removed his own gag and Jerry didn't seem to care. His hands were still tied at the wrist making it hard to finger the cards. They used IOU's penciled on scraps of paper. Tait got ahead by a hundred dollars and Jerry couldn't resist increasing the stakes even though the game was of no consequence.

Katie was on her side sleeping on the floor. Marcus, leaning against the wall, pulled down his gag and asked, "What day is it?"

"Friday," Tait answered.

Marcus yelled at Jerry, "You won't get away with this you stinking pig. My mom and dad will be looking for me."

"Your folks will find you, alright. Dead!" Jerry said with a smirk and went over and placed the gag back on Marcus.

"You're too mouthy, kid. I like it quiet," he said as he smacked Marcus on the back of the head and laughed, amusing himself.

"Criminals always take something or leave something at the scene of the crime," Tait said attempting to negotiate their release. "A police officer told me that. You will get caught. You might leave a fingerprint or ..."

"Oh, just shut up," Jerry demanded. "You think you're smart, don't you kid. Well, I'm smart too. For your information my name is not Jerry. Nobody around here knows my real name."

"Really! What is it?"

"Ed," he said instinctively and then frowned at his own careless mistake. "I'm not telling you my last name."

"Short for Edgar I suppose," Tait said trying to use tack to get him to reveal more.

"Heck no," he said laughing. "Now that's funny."

"Edward then."

"No."

"Edwin," Tait said spurring him on.

"No."

"Edwood."

"It's short for Eddy. Now shut up and play cards or I'll gag you again.

Katie began to sob so Tait hobbled over to her side

and spoke in her ear.

"Cyrum has always come through. Don't give up. He will get us out of this," he assured her.

"But he is dead," she cried beginning to sob again.

"Cyrum is tough. He is a warrior. I've seen him in action and I know he is one bad dude when he's mad. No little bullet is going to stop him."

Katie's face was streaked with tears yet she nodded in agreement. Cyrum would save them.

The day wore on dull and boring. The kids dozed often. Darkness crept upon them gradually, almost unnoticed.

A bang on the back door woke them up. Mr. Wiggleshoes had returned but didn't enter fast like the last time. He didn't want to startle Jerry. He might shoot him.

"Where have you been partner?" Jerry asked. "It's been a long day."

Mr. Wiggleshoes ignored the comment and simply said, "The maintenance worker will be here with the diamond at 9:00 P.M. sharp. I have your cash, ten thousand dollars."

"Let me see it," Jerry said getting up from the table.

"You'll see it soon enough. His instructions were to enter the house from the rear. Keep a look out."

Mr. Wiggleshoes opened his black briefcase. He pulled out a black felt cloth and placed it on the table. A battery with curly copper terminals on top was pulled out of the briefcase and set on the table. A fluorescent lamp on a stand was then placed by the cloth along with a magnifying glass, a jeweler's saw, and other things useful for examining a diamond. Stacks of twenty dollar bills could be seen neatly placed in rows in the suitcase. Wires from the lamp were hooked up to the battery and the lamp turned on.

"Hey, that works pretty good," the bum said. "You got a sandwich in that briefcase."

"You can eat all you want when this meeting is over."

Katie sat up and spoke through her gag which had loosened its grip. "Oh, Tait, I'm so hungry."

"I've got a headache like you wouldn't believe," Marcus muttered as he sat up. His eyes were puffy and he slowly slumped down on his side again, worn out.

Tait was exhausted also, but was not willing to accept defeat. All he needed was a break; he was still waiting for his opportunity.

Wiggleshoes was nervous. He got up from the chair and paced the room and then sat down again. He looked at his watch and said, "He ought to be here any minute now." He rearranged the objects on the table, moving the lamp a little to the left, and then smoothing out the cloth upon which he was going to place the diamond for examination.

Jerry came into the kitchen from the pantry and informed Mr. Wiggleshoes that a man was out back in the yard. Mr. Wiggleshoes got up and looked through the back-door window.

"That's him. Let him in," he said.

The man came in and stood in the kitchen looking at the kids.

"What are they doing here?"

"They know you stole the diamond and how you did it. They were following me around so I nabbed them.

I'll take care of them so don't worry about it," Mr. Wiggleshoes explained.

"I stole the diamond but I'll take no part in murder," the guy said.

"You don't have to. Did you bring it?"

He pulled out a handkerchief and unwrapped it. Tait watched as the man give the Hope Diamond to Mr. Wiggleshoes who quickly sat down at the table and put the diamond under the white light. Mr. Wiggleshoes looked up at Jerry.

"Get these kids out of here."

Jerry dragged Marcus into the bathroom and then came and got Katie. Tait was up on his feet and hopped his way into the room. Tait positioned himself by the open door so he could see what was taking place. Jerry then returned to the table and sat down with his elbows on the table and chin in his hands, looking tired.

The maintenance man had his head next to Mr. Wiggleshoes looking at the Hope Diamond under the light of the lamp. Mr. Wiggleshoes had a magnifying glass and was examining the diamond. The three men sat around the table not as friends, but as lions all chewing on the same carcass and willing to bite anyone who tried to take more than his share.

"This diamond was owned by King Louis XIV of France in 1668," Mr. Wiggleshoes explained. It was mined in India. The diamond was stolen in 1792 and turned up in London. Its history is fascinating. Gentlemen, I will now be part of that history. At my death when this jewel is discovered among my inventory, I will become world renowned and part of the fabulous history of this most famous gem."

"You can have your history. We'll have the money. We want to live like King Louis now," the man said.

"Just a minute. I want to make sure this is not a fraud. You are thieves and not to be trusted, am I correct?" he said smiling at them in jest.

The man laughed. "It's the real thing. Maybe I should check out the green bills you have in your briefcase. You are a thief and not to be trusted," he said throwing the comment right back at Wiggleshoes.

"Sit down and have a look. Count it if you like.

It's all there."

"Yes, but are they counterfeit bills?"

Mr. Wiggleshoes gave them a glaring stare but then quietly continued to examine the Blue Diamond with intense interest.

The two men began counting the money. Jerry grabbed a bundle of money, too, and began counting out his share.

Tait stood up and started to make his way out of the bathroom in an effort to escape. The three men were engrossed in their exploits and not paying attention to the kids.

"Hey! Jerry! I told you to get those kids out of here. Take them upstairs to the bedroom. The windows are all boarded up. There is no way of escape up there."

Jerry grabbed Tait and pushed him toward the stairs, making him fall. Jerry took out a pocket knife and slashed the ankle cords.

"Get up," he demanded and poked Tait in the hip with the point of his knife. He went over and picked up the camper's lantern off the table and then cut the ankle cords from around the other two and then herded all three kids up the stairs. The kids were pushed through the bedroom door one at a time and the door closed. They stood in the dark room gagged and tied at the wrist. They heard Jerry walk back down the steps.

Tait removed his gag. "We can still get out of here," Tait announced. "Marcus give me your hands." Tait worked on untying Marcus' hands. The knot was tight. He used his teeth to pull the knot apart. It was dark and everything was done blind. When they were all untied, the three kids stood in the room with nowhere to go. They heard the men coming up the stairs.

"Just throw the lantern on the bed. It will go up in flames like a match," they heard one of the men say.

The door opened and the lantern flew onto the bed. The bed burst into flames and the room lit up from the fire.

"Drop to the floor," Tait yelled out. "If you catch on fire, roll."

Tait tugged on the door but it was locked.

"Crawl to the window. Let's try and tear off the

plywood and get air," Tait directed.

Tait and Marcus succeeded in getting enough of the plywood loose for them to breath. They heard a lot of hollering from outside. Men yelled, "Police! Police! Get down on the ground. Spread your legs."

"Hey buddy! You can't go in there!" Tait heard one of the police officers scream.

They heard someone dashing and stumbling up the steps and then the door slammed open.

"It's me, Cyrum! Are you kids in there?"

In unison they all screamed. "Cyrum!"

Running he threw his body at the plywood covering the window. It gave way to fresh air and light as he landed on the front porch roof.

Tait shoved Katie out the window and then Marcus stuck his leg through the opening, forcing Tait to do a head-roll onto the porch roof.

They all sucked in the fresh air and gazed at the flashing lights.

"I'm feeling a little weak," Katie said shakily. Tait moved over and held her up.

"We'll be home soon," he said. "Be tough."

Marcus rolled over on his back, spread his arms and legs out like he was on a beach, in no hurry to move.

"Look!" Tait pointed in the direction of the street. "The police officer is shoving Mr. Wiggleshoes into the back of his cruiser.

Chapter 14

The Reunion

Smoke poured out of the upstairs windows around the plywood coverings. Sirens were heard from a long way off coming from different directions. The angle of the roof caused Tait's knees to buckle to keep his balance. He saw one huge ladder truck come around the corner, blowing its siren one last time before coming to a stop. It woke up the neighbors.

Tait stood motionless observing fire fighters. Each one had a particular duty. Water hose lines the size of python snakes quickly covered the ground. Two of them wasted no time erecting a ladder to the porch roof. One man stayed at the bottom while the other climbed to the roof.

"Are there any more people in the house?" the fire fighter hollered up at Tait.

"There is no one left in the house," answered Tait.

These two wore fire resistant suits with oxygen tanks on their backs. They helped the kids down the ladder and questioned them as to their health.

Other fire fighters rushed up on the roof and used their axes to remove the plywood from windows. Tait observed a fire fighter kneeling on the roof, holding onto a water hose, keeping it under control while his partner shot water into the burning building through a window.

The blaze lit up the sky and the fire fighters worked fast and hard to get the blaze under control. The fire was contained promptly and did not spread to nearby houses. Neighbors were out on the sidewalks in their pajamas gazing at the fire.

Cyrum had a white bandage around his head. His left ear bulged from the padding.

"What happened to your head?" Tait asked.

"I got shot. My dog was injured too."

"Is the bullet stuck in your head?" Marcus asked, viewing the massive head bandage.

"No, the bullet just grazed me. Part of my left ear took stitches. I'll be all right."

"What about your dog? Is he okay?" Katie asked.

"Yes, my dog is okay. He got shot in the muscle of his hind-leg. He is recovering nicely.

"Marcus gave up on you but I didn't," Katie informed Cyrum.

"I didn't either," Marcus chimed in defending himself. "Why didn't you show up at Wympee's?"

"So you lost hope in me?" Cyrum said, sporting with Marcus. "Do you remember seeing a big lady in the restaurant with a man in a Red's ball cap?"

"Yeah," Marcus answered slowly, trying to figure out the connection.

"I was the big lady in disguise. I was working undercover."

"That was you?" said a surprised Tait. "Why

didn't you say something earlier?"

"I didn't want to blow my cover in front of Jerry. I waited until you were leaving. I waved for you to stop but you took off."

"Did you see the Cadillac chase us down Wayne Avenue," Tait asked.

"Yes, I did. I followed that Cadillac to the cemetary in my car and waited for it to come out again, which it did. You kids were in the back. I was surprised when the Cadillac went to the railroad bridge after dark. Fortunately, Joey is an undercover police officer."

"Who is Joey?" Katie asked.

"The little man in the Cincinnati baseball cap that was with me in the restaurant."

"That little guy is a cop!" Marcus mused, amazed.

"Yep! He's the one that informed your parents and his department downtown. The whole police force was looking for you kids."

A large police officer guided the children to the back seat of his cruiser.

"What about our bikes?" Tait asked the officer.

"Where are they?"

"In the back of the Cadillac," Tait informed the officer.

The bicycles were removed from the Cadillac and placed in the trunk of the police cruiser. On the way home, Tait realizing he would have to face his parents, discussed how his dad would be furious that he didn't know anything about what was going on. Marcus always seemed to get off easy while Tait would get grounded or get chores to do.

"Oh, Katie!" Her mother whispered into her ear as she crushed her with a welcome home hug. "I was so worried about you."

Tait stood silently inside the front door, waiting for his dad to pronounce the punishment. To his surprise, Tait received a long, strong hug from his dad.

"I'm glad you're home safe, son," Tait's dad said. "I think maybe you learned a valuable lesson today."

"Yeah, I did. I meant to come to you and Mom after meeting Cyrum at Wympee's but everything went wrong."

"Next time, you come to me early before you get involved in dangerous activity," scolded his Dad while shaking Tait's shoulder with affection.

Tait's dad had a long talk with Cyrum and the police officer while Mom made chicken noodle soup and peanut butter sandwiches, a befitting "prodigal son" meal.

Next day, Tait was quick to retrieve the morning paper and sure enough, their story made the front page.

"The Hope Diamond case solved," the headlines read. "Three area youths sleuth out the case with the help of Cyrum T. Washington, a former World War II pilot. The children were kidnapped and set to be murdered in a house fire. Cyrum with the aid of police, rescued the kids and captured Mr. Wiggleshoes, a well known local gemologist. A waste treatment plant worker and a transient also were booked on charges of theft and attempted murder."

Tait was shocked to read another article also on the front page of the paper down in the left-hand corner.

A reunion of the black airmen had been scheduled at the University of Dayton on June 15. The names of those to be honored were listed and Cyrum T. Washington was among them.

Cyrum called later that week and surprised them by inviting all the kids to accompany him to the reunion.

Arriving at the reunion and entering the banquet hall, Tait thought it the largest banquet he had ever attended. There were a hundred round-top tables with white tablecloths and flower centerpieces scattered throughout the auditorium. The kids walked into the banquet hall with Cyrum's family.

"Hey," Marcus hollered softly in the direction of Tait. "Our names are on the table." Each seat had a white cardboard nameplate on the table with their names printed in bold black letters.

"Mind your manners," Katie told the boys. "Eat with your forks. No fingers."

A place setting with knives, forks, napkins and fancy plates was on the table in front of each of the eight soft chairs that surrounded it. Coffee cups were upside down on saucers by the silverware. Crystal water glasses sparkled. Each table had a number in the center and under the numbers were the words, "By Request". The kids sat at table number nine with Cyrum's brother Jim and Dennis Tucker.

"What does "By Request" mean? Tait asked.

Dennis explained, "It is in memory of the fact that the white bomber pilots, selected to fly a dangerous bombing mission over Germany, requested the black airmen to escort them for protection."

Cyrum sat at the head table with the other notable flyers. The head table at the front of the auditorium was twenty-feet long for the guests of honor. A lot of the men and women in attendance wore military uniforms. The room was crowded with clusters of people talking to one another, patting each other on the back, joking and laughing. One lady screamed when she recognized someone she knew and hadn't seen in a long time.

A trumpet sounded a few notes and everyone went to his or her assigned seats. All the people stood at attention behind their chairs. The Air Force military band played the National Anthem. Those in uniform saluted the flag while most put their hands over their hearts. It was like a prayer time, serious and very emotional. Some cried.

Everyone was commenting on the fabulous meal. Katie cut her chicken cordon bleu and asked Marcus what he was eating.

"Meat," he said.

"Looks like filet mignon steak to me. Do you like it?"

"I was hoping for a hamburger and fries."

"Don't be silly. Wait until the dessert comes. You'll like it."

Dessert came and Marcus said it was some sort of fake ice cream. Katie corrected him and said it was Sherbet.

The conversation at the table eventually got around to the Hope Diamond. Tait mentioned that the Hope Diamond was no longer going to be shown at exhibits around the world. An announcement had been made that on November 10, 1958, the Harry Winston company, was formally going to donate the Hope Diamond to the Smithsonian Institution.

A lady at the head table hit her wineglass with a spoon and got everyone's attention.

"It's time we acknowledged our men and women in uniform," she said. She went to the podium and introduced a black general who gave a long speech.

Cyrum's turn came and he was introduced as one of the most decorated pilots in the air command.

Cyrum stood up and said, "My wounded spirit is beginning to mend. War causes internal pain." His voice cracked with a hint of sorrow at the thought of it all. Removing a folded piece of paper out of his wallet, Cyrum cleared his throat and read a poem from it written in pencil.

Hope

Death looks me in the face

I fly tomorrow

Will I return an Ace

or will I bring sorrow

Don't be blue

Love lives forever

What is important to me is inportant to you

that's what holds us together

Love is the glue that binds men

no matter how different on the outside

So I will love you friend

and not die on the inside

Jesus did not lie

He will save our lives

Don't cry

It's not goodbye

Love will not die

I'm going up high

to say to God hi

Hope don't sigh

"Dan gave me his poem before he went out on his fatal last mission. I lost my zest for life. I couldn't see a bright future. I couldn't even vote when I got back home. I got my hope restored. The poem speaks of the hope of eternal life.

President Harry Truman issued two executive orders in 1948 ending discrimination in the armed forces and civilian agencies of the federal government. Then in 1954 the Brown school-desegregation decision opened up all schools to black children. Last year, in 1956, a Supreme Court decision banned segregated busing. I'm no longer a second class citizen. The Air Force has been a good family to me.

I realized that it is our relationships with God and people that are important. Our lives influence others. The equality of treatment, our new opportunities in this country to succeed, and the children of America give me hope.

I would like to introduce to you today three children who fought for justice and won. They were instrumental in recovering the Hope Diamond. Tait, Marcus, and Katie please stand and receive a warm welcome."

Cyrum sat down with cheers that lasted so long that people decided to stand up and clap.

Later, an executive came up to Cyrum and patted him on the back, surprising Cyrum with a job offer. He needed someone to fly commercial aircraft from Dayton to other parts of the U.S. Cyrum was delighted. The celebration gave renewed hope to everyone. The kids left early. The adults stayed well-past midnight.

Tait and Katie didn't get grounded. The close shave with death was lesson enough. According to his dad, Tait took too many risks and endangered Katie and Marcus. But Tait was not specifically prohibited from playing detective.

Tait found two flat twelve-inch wooden rulers in the house and painted them black. With the skill of an artist he painted the letters of three words in white. Katie, Marcus and Tait hung the sign with a chain over the lantern style garage light. The sign swung gently in the wind. "Detectives for hire."